Undercover Heat

JUDY MAYS

An Ellora's Cave Romantica Publication

www.ellorascave.com

Undercover Heat

ISBN 9781419961472

Edited by Raelene Gorlinsky.
Cover art by Syneca.

This book printed in the U.S.A. by Jasmine-Jade Enterprises, LLC.

Electronic book publication April 2010
Trade paperback publication September 2010

UNDERCOVER HEAT

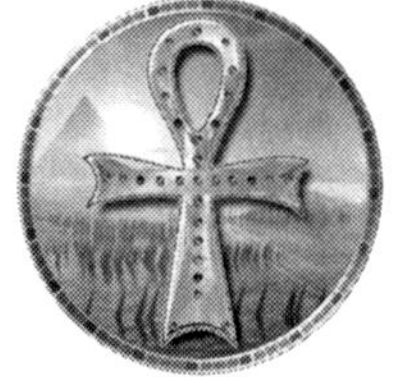

Dedication

ꕥ

For Mom and Dad

Chapter One

ଛ

Clad in loose camouflage pants and a tight, black tee shirt, he shoved the door open and swaggered into her inner office as if he owned the place.

"Are you Melody Gray?"

The arrogance in his tone sent enough of a surge of adrenalin pulsing through Melody's veins to hack away at her fatigue. Blinking to clear her blurred vision, she almost curled her lip—almost. Arrogance in a human was hard to stomach because none of them were as tough as they thought they were. But he was a potential client and she preferred to pay her own way in the world rather than live off her father's money.

When he cleared his throat loudly, more irritation surfaced. How the hell did he get in here, anyway? Where was John? He was supposed to keep jerks like this out of her office.

Her stomach growled and she remembered. He was getting her something to eat.

Squaring her shoulders, Melody raked her hair back over her forehead. Damn, but she was exhausted. She needed to sleep, but now she had to make nice to a customer. She blinked again and looked up.

Her gaze got as far as his mouth.

He had a superior sneer on his lips.

Biting the inside of her mouth to control her own expression, Melody did her best to swallow her immediate dislike and forced a blank look onto her face. What a jerk! She wasn't going to like this one at all.

Dropping a glance to the manila folder he carried, she

pushed herself to her feet and held out her hand. "What can I do for you, Mr....?"

He ignored it. "Nick Price, CIA. You look like hell."

Anger flared as Melody glared up into his coffee-colored face. This guy wasn't just an arrogant jerk, he was a bona fide asshole. "Listen, Nick Price of the fucking CIA—if you're telling me the truth. Since when did CIA agents start wearing camo instead of cheap, black suits?"

"Not that it's any of your business, but I've been undercover."

"Well, I just spent the last forty-eight hours with only a couple hours of sleep searching for a twelve-year-old runaway who thought she could survive in the wilds of Nevada. So, up yours, shithead, and don't let the door hit you in the ass on the way out."

"Do you kiss your mother with that mouth?" He flashed his badge at her then tossed a picture from the folder onto her desk. "I'm looking for this man."

Melody stared at the blurry photograph on her desk and tried to refocus her gaze. Christ, a fucking government spook. That *was* a real CIA badge he just flashed at her, wasn't it? What the hell did he want? She was in no shape to match wits with him now. She was just too tired.

"My mother's dead."

"I'm sorry." He didn't look or sound the least bit sorry.

He pointed at the picture. "Have you seen that guy?"

Picking up the photo, she blinked some more to focus, and stared at it. "Yeah, I've seen him. What do you want him for?"

She never looked up, but his subtle foot shuffle and slight intake of breath told her that wasn't the answer he expected. Grinning to herself, she dropped the picture on her desk. Ha! He didn't expect her to admit it. "Said his name was Jake Fields. He came in wanting to hire us to find his wife. Said she took off with a pile of his money," she said.

The CIA spook pressed his palms against her desk and leaned forward. "His real name is Jake Hurley, and he's wanted on suspicion of treason. Any idea where he is now?"

She inhaled slowly. His scent was completely masculine. No fruity cologne for him. As her werewolf soul struggled to shake off its fatigue, Melody fought keep her wits functioning. When she looked into his face, the werewolf in her soul stirred for a moment.

Something in his eyes…

Melody blinked again. Exhaustion settled more firmly around her shoulders and weighed her down. Her werewolf soul sighed and fell into a deep slumber.

"It was our money. You gonna help me or not?" His voice was terse, and he didn't bother hiding his irritation.

Dropping her gaze to the sneer on his lips, she pushed the picture back across her desk. He'd have some inane answer for any question she asked. And she was too tired to ask anymore. "My partner worked with him. When John gets back from lunch, I'll see what he remembers. Come back tomorrow, and we'll give you everything we have on him." *After I've had some sleep and am able to think again.*

Price picked up the photo, stared at her a moment, and nodded. "I'll be in touch." Spinning on his heel, he sauntered out of her office.

Melody didn't move until he'd cleared the outer office and disappeared through the door to the street.

Flopping into her chair, she stared at the opposite wall, though she didn't see the pictures hanging there. Jerking a drawer open, she pulled out a cell phone and punched in her father's private number.

Her brother Garth's spook had just traced him to her.

Chapter Two

ꟹ

With the aroma of fresh-washed pine and wet forest loam surrounding him, Nick leaned back against the tree and tried to settle into a more comfortable position on the damp ground. Bits and pieces of broken shale from an old rockslide lay scattered around and underneath the pine tree where he'd concealed himself. It made for uncomfortable sitting and his ass was getting cold as the seat of his pants absorbed moisture from the pine needles beneath him, but this spot afforded the best view through the large front window of Melody Gray's cabin. Besides, he'd conducted surveillance in worse places. At least he wasn't hiding in an open sewer or a sand mound full of ants. He shifted off a pointy stone and focused his binoculars on the cabin.

After leaving Gray's office earlier that day, he'd wandered down the street, leaned against a lamp pole, and watched her front door until her partner returned. After giving them ten minutes, he'd sauntered back to the office. No way was he waiting until tomorrow to give them time to destroy what could be incriminating evidence. When he'd walked in, the inner door to her office was closed, but her partner John had been more than affable. After Nick identified himself, Gray's partner had pulled a file out of a drawer, copied everything right there in front of Nick, and handed it to him in a new manila folder. Then he'd wished Nick luck finding Fields. Though Nick had wished to confront Gray again, he hadn't been able to do more than thank her partner and leave. John had stood with legs spread and arms crossed over his chest almost as if he had been daring Nick to try to get past him.

The roar of a powerful motor pulled Nick from his

thoughts, and he focused his binoculars on the dirt road leading to the cabin. As Melody Gray's green SUV appeared over the crest of the hill and skidded to a stop next to the cabin, Nick mulled over the information he'd read in the file he'd gotten from Gray's partner. It seemed as if they had given him everything. All the information about the man they knew as Jake Fields was there—from the date he'd first hired their agency to the date he'd terminated their employment. Every hour they'd billed him was accounted for—trips to other towns to gather evidence, records searches, surveillance, everything. Nothing there indicated that Jake Fields aka Jake Hurley was anything more to them than a client who'd employed them for two weeks.

But…

Refocusing his binoculars as Melody Gray slid out of her vehicle and headed to the side door of her cabin, Nick concentrated on her. She stumbled once, caught herself, shifted the backpack she carried to her other shoulder then wearily climbed the two steps to the porch and disappeared from his view when she entered her cabin.

Frowning, Nick refocused on the large window at the front of her house and waited for her to reappear. Nothing about her, this town, or the information he'd received said her connection to the man he was hunting was anything other than what she'd revealed to him. He had no reason to be here. He should be off hunting his quarry.

Except…

Melody Gray was lying.

His gut told him so and his gut was never wrong.

All of the information in the file was neat, legible, and logical—too neat, too legible, too logical. He'd stake his professional reputation on it. All he had to do was keep her under surveillance until he figured out why she was protecting Hurley. If he was right about her lying, and he was sure he was, sooner or later she'd lead him to the man his boss swore was a werewolf.

A squirrel sitting on a branch above him chattered in disgust and scrambled away—sending a shower of cold raindrops down onto his head and shoulders. Nick muttered a vehement curse about his superior's parentage. Werewolf! Emil Sorescu was a fucking idiot. He'd sworn Nick to secrecy when he called him into his office—before assigning this job. At first, Nick had contemplated revealing his assignment to Sorescu's superiors but then decided against it. Officially, Nick was looking for possible terrorists who'd sneaked into the United States across the Canadian border and were waiting for instructions about where to attack. If Nick tried to tell anyone Sorescu had him chasing after a werewolf, his boss would certainly deny everything. Then Nick would be the one looking like a fucking idiot. What's more, Sorescu had enough pull to have Nick riding a desk for the next twenty years. Being stuck in an office every day would drive him crazy.

Nick shifted again to relax a cramped muscle. A bird landed on a slender branch above him, and more icy water drops rolled down the back of his neck. Christ, what a farce! This was the stupidest fucking assignment he'd ever had. As soon as he dragged Hurley in, he was transferring to another department as far away from his idiotic boss as he could get. Sooner or later, the asshole was going to crack and do something really crazy to screw up a case, and Nick didn't plan to be anywhere near him to be dragged down in his wake. Nope, Nick Price was going to cover his own ass.

Shifting off yet another sharp rock that was jabbing his calf, Nick muttered another curse but kept his binoculars trained on his quarry as Melody Gray walked into her living room. There, she stripped her tee shirt over her head, dropped it to the floor, and headed through the doorway that led to her bedroom, which was also located in the front of the cabin.

Nick leaned forwarded and readjusted his binoculars. He'd scouted Gray's cabin from the outside before she'd come home. She had a very good security system installed, though he was confident that he could bypass the code whenever he wanted. He hadn't bothered because he knew he didn't have time to get in, search as much as he wanted to, and then get out before she came home. For now, it was enough that the living room and her bedroom were at the front of the house, with curtains that were pulled back from the windows of both. Though the bedroom window wasn't as large as that in the living room, he still had a good view of what she did as she moved from one room to the next.

In the bedroom, she slipped out of her jeans then stripped off her bra and panties. In a small corner of his mind, Nick noted that they were white cotton. Grannie panties. Yep, she was probably as frigid as her silver-blonde hair. One question that had surfaced in his mind about her, though, was answered when she turned around and stretched. Her cunt hair was the same silvery color as that on her head. She was a natural blonde. His gaze wandered back up to her breasts. Her nipples were pink! Fuck, but he'd never seen a woman with pink nipples.

Then he shook his head. "Shit, Price," he mumbled to himself. "Who cares? You're not here to screw her, you're here to do a job. Do it."

He conquered the slight stirring in his groin as he continued to watch his quarry.

When she flopped down naked onto her bed and didn't move, Nick let his binoculars drop to hang by the strap against his chest. He'd done some checking around town before coming out here. A teenage girl *had* been lost in the mountains, and Melody Gray *had* been part of the search party that spent two days looking for her, so she'd been telling the truth when she'd said she was exhausted. Gray wouldn't be going anywhere for the next twelve to fourteen hours, which gave him plenty of time to search and bug her office tonight. If he didn't find what he wanted there, he'd bug her house in a day or so.

As he rose, the feeling that he was being watched had the

hairs on the back on his neck standing straight up. Pulling his revolver from its holster beneath his coat, he whirled. The mottled gray wolf that had been watching him leaped into the bushes and disappeared.

A runnel of sweat rolled down the side of his head.

Werewolf? Was it possible?

"Christ, Price," he growled to the empty air, "get a hold of yourself. That fucking idiot Sorescu is getting to you. It was just a wolf."

When the wolf didn't reappear, Nick holstered his gun, put his binoculars in their case and headed up to the access road where he'd parked his jeep. Werewolves were figments of his boss's imagination, fictional creations of the knuckleheads in Hollywood or those horny, middle-aged women who wrote romance novels, just like vampires were. Hell, right now he was in the middle of freakin' nowhere, and everybody knew wolves were returning to remote places in the Rocky Mountains—if they had ever completely left. From everything he'd read, and he'd read a lot about wolves since he'd received this assignment, they pretty much stayed as far away from humans as they could. The wolf he'd just seen had probably stumbled across him purely by chance. The wind was blowing the wrong way for it to catch his scent, or it would have avoided him altogether. It was a real wolf. Werewolves just didn't exist.

After trudging steadily upward for twenty minutes, Nick reached his vehicle. Once he stowed his gear, he climbed in, did a three-point turn, and headed back down the mountain. When he was finished bugging Gray's office, he could head back to his motel for a couple hours of shuteye.

From the cover of thick pine trees, the large, gray wolf sniffed the air and watched the jeep disappear down the mountain. Curling his lips back, he snarled. He would not forget this human's scent.

Chapter Three

ꟗ

Melody was sleeping like a baby, her arms wrapped around a pillow when he slipped into her bedroom. For a moment, he simply stared at her. Then he grinned slyly. This was a perfect chance for a little revenge. Spinning on his heel, he headed into the bathroom and returned a minute later with a glass of water.

"Wake up, Sunshine. Are you going to sleep the day away?" With those words, he dribbled water into her face.

She woke up flailing her arms and legs and cursing. "What the hell…" Blinking water out of her eyes, she focus on him then snapped, "Brendan, you jerk! What did you do that for?"

Brendan simply grinned at his sister's struggles, sure that only the sheet tangled around her legs kept her from jumping him. "Payback can be a bitch, and I owed you," he answered as he backed away. She was getting untangled, and being tackled by Melody usually turned out to be very painful. Just like their sister Belle, Melody never showed any hesitation in an attack—and she was stronger and harder than their baby sister. Garth was the only one of her three brothers she'd never beaten in a fight, and that was only because he weighed a good hundred pounds more than she did.

"Notice I didn't throw the entire glass on you like I should have. Once you dumped a whole bucket of water on me."

Combing her hair back off her forehead with her fingers, she growled, "That's because it was for both you and Garth, and he's so damn big, I needed the whole bucket. Besides, you hardly got wet 'cause you heard me coming."

Brendan set the glass on the dresser. She was getting a golden glint in her eyes and her form was beginning to blur. Best to change the subject. "Why were you sleeping like the dead? Anybody could have come in here."

"Like hell, brother mine. You're the only person other than me who knows the security code for my alarm system, which *is* loud enough to wake the dead." Finally untangled from the bedding, she rose to her feet and reached for her robe. Unlike humans, werewolves weren't uncomfortable nude, but mornings in the mountains were cool. "I should kick your ass from here to Idaho and back."

"Forget that," Brendan said gesturing toward the robe she lifted from the bottom of the bed. "Come run with me. We haven't raced through the forest together in a long time."

Tilting her head, Melody smiled as the irritation she felt for her brother melted away. Brendan was right. She hadn't run with him, or any other member of her family, in a long time, something she missed more than she liked to admit. "I'd love to, let's go."

Silver mist swirled where Brendan had been standing and almost immediately dissipated. A large silver-gray wolf stood in his place—with a red tee shirt completely enveloping his head.

Melody burst into laughter. "Idiot! That's what you get for trying to show off. Dad's the only one who can shift out of his clothes."

After using his paws to pull the shirt off his head, the wolf glared at her. *Garth can, too. And do you think Dad got it right the first time? Practice makes perfect, you know. Now hurry up and shift so we can run. I've been itching to get into the forest.*

"Outside," Melody answered as she led the way through the living room. "I want to set the alarm again."

Problems?

She shrugged as she shut her front door and enabled the alarm system. "I don't know. There was a CIA agent in my office looking for Garth, though he didn't know his real name. I gave him the fake file I had, but I don't think he believed it."

One of the reasons I'm here. Dad got your message.

She stared at her brother. "I just phoned Dad yesterday. You couldn't have gotten here from New York that fast. Since when did werewolves grow wings?"

Light glinted on white fangs as Brendan opened his mouth in what could only be a laugh. *I was already at Belle's so I didn't have as far to travel.*

More silvery mist sparkled as Melody shifted into a white wolf. *Can't catch me,* she sent to her brother and leaped toward the forest.

With a happy yelp, Brendan leaped after her. Gods, how he wished all his siblings were here so they could run together. It had been far too long since they'd run as a pack.

Hours later, tongue lolling, he followed his sister into a small clearing where the sweet scent of fresh water permeated the air. They'd run mile after mile, chasing deer, rabbits and a two-year-old black bear for the simple joy of it. More than once, Melody had howled from the sheer delight of running free, and chills had shot up and down Brendan's backbone. Never in all his travels had he encountered either a *Were* or a full wolf with a voice as lovely as hers. Their father had told them their mother's voice had been beautiful, and the first time he'd heard Melody's infant howl, he'd known her voice would be the same. That's why he'd named her Melody.

After letting his sister drink from the small stream, Brendan dipped his head and began to lap thirstily. It was pure instinct that made him leap back when the strange wolf catapulted across the stream. Still, Brendan wasn't quite quick enough. The other wolf's teeth missed him, but its shoulder hit Brendan's side, and he was knocked from his feet. Scrambling up, he turned to face his attacker. Baring his teeth, he growled a warning. He didn't want to fight a Forest Brother, but he would if he had to.

Snarling thunderously, a large, mottled-gray wolf faced him, its yellow eyes burning with anger.

Brendan never took his own stare from the other male. Christ, but this one must really be territorial. Obviously, he and Melody weren't going to be able to talk their way out of a fight. Oh well, with his sister's help, he'd be able to subdue this wolf without inflicting too much damage—he hoped.

Before the other wolf could charge, however, Melody shifted and stepped between them. "Damn it, Drake, stop it."

The other wolf's eyes never left Brendan as he answered her. *You are mine. This male has no right to you.*

Before Brendan could react to that comment, his sister fisted her hands on her hips and glared at the big gray wolf. "This male is my brother, my sibling, my littermate. Damn it, even male *wolves* are idiots!"

The wild wolf stopped snarling and shifted his gaze to Melody's face. *He is your sibling?*

"That's what I just said, asshole."

The insult was completely lost on the wolf. Licking the saliva from his lips, he sat back on his haunches and bowed his head. *My apologies, sibling of my mate. I did not know.*

Shifting to human, Brendan crossed his arms over his chest and turned his full attention on his sister. "Mate? Is there something you haven't told the family, Melody?"

Cursing long and loudly, Melody spun on her heel and stomped to the other side of the small clearing. Then she pivoted and stomped back. "Damn it, Drake, you pig-headed, idiotic, moronic, ass! I am *not* your mate. I do *not* want to be your mate. I am *not* going to spend the rest of my life living in the woods without bubble baths, football, and chocolate. How many times do I have to tell you? No! No! No! I *will not* be your mate!"

Her brother looked down at the wolf. "That sounds like no to me."

The wolf looked up at Brendan. *I do not understand her. I do not have the head of a pig. Nor do I look like a donkey. And I don't know what kind of animals idiotics or moronics are, and she will not tell me.*

"Oooo! Pain-in-the-ass, cock-sucking shithead!" Stomping her foot and trailing another string of curses behind her, Melody spun and retreated to the other side of the clearing again. Hearing her brother chuckle only made her angrier. Damn that wolf Drake! Why couldn't he take *no* for an answer? She didn't want to be his mate, now or ever. He wasn't the male for her. Now, if he had rocked her world when she looked into his eyes, she wouldn't have thought twice about joining him, even if it meant giving up chocolate. But—he didn't. The werewolf in her soul didn't howl with joy whenever Drake showed up. Maybe Brendan could convince him to leave her alone.

Spinning once again, she glared at her brother. "Would you please tell him I don't want to be his mate! He won't listen to me."

Instead of the sympathy she expected, Brendan grinned. "I don't know, Mel. He's a pretty well-set-up wolf. You could do worse."

As her mouth dropped open, he continued, "And you know how tenacious wolves are. My telling him to leave you alone isn't going to work. You just have to be patient. He'll get tired of waiting for you—eventually."

Snapping her mouth shut, Melody sputtered for a few minutes. Then, "Males! You are both idiots! I'm going home." Silvery mist swirled again, and the white wolf that was Melody sprinted south.

When the gray wolf made to follow her, Brendan grabbed him by the scruff of the neck and pulled him back only to release him as soon as he bared his teeth and turned to bite. Throwing his hands up, Brendan said, "My apologies, Forest Brother, but if you continue to harass my sibling, I will have to defend her."

The wolf stared at him with a level yellow gaze. *The Laws of the Pack allow me to court any unmated female I wish. She is not only unmated but she also left her natal pack a long time ago. Even as her sibling, you do not have the right to deny me. Have you lived among the humans so long that you've forgotten the Laws?*

Brendan shook his head. "I have not forgotten, Forest Brother, but living among humans has brought me and all of my siblings closer than is usual. We still fight for each other no matter how many miles separate us."

The wolf cocked his head to the side for a moment. *I will acknowledge this if you acknowledge my right to court her.*

Sighing, Brendan raked the fingers of both hands through his hair. According to the Fourth Law of the Pack, the wolf did have the right since both were unmated. Hopefully, Melody's rebuffs would soon work, and this male would seek a mate somewhere else. "I acknowledge your right."

Rising to his feet, the wolf nodded. *Good. I will leave you to your reunion with your sibling—for now. But I will return to her.*

"So be it," Brendan said as he prepared to shift.

One other thing, Were.

Brendan stared into the wolf's golden eyes.

There was a man watching her log cave yesterday.

Brendan stiffened. "What man?"

I never smelled him before, but he sat among the pines on the hill and looked down into her den with a black object he held before his eyes. Hoping I would scare him away, I allowed him to see me. He had one of the sticks that spits fire and death so I hid from him. I do not think I succeeded in my attempt to frighten him.

"Fuck!" Brendan growled mostly to himself. Then, looking at the wolf, he bowed his head. "My thanks, Forest Brother. Stay away from this man, for he is dangerous."

I will protect my mate.

Exhaling slowly, Brendan shook his head. He was beginning to understand why Melody was so obviously frustrated with this particular wolf. “I will pass your warning on to her.” Mist swirled, and the silvery-gray wolf that was Brendan leaped in the general direction Melody had taken.

Drake watched him disappear. This wolf was lucky he was Melody’s sibling, otherwise he would be a very dead wolf right now. Throwing back his head, Drake let loose a long, lonely howl. Too many seasons now, he’d been alone. Melody would fill the emptiness in his heart. He was sure of it.

Chapter Four

ℬ

Dust motes danced in the rays of the sun as Melody slammed the side door open and stomped through her kitchen and living room into her bedroom. Damn that boneheaded Drake! He was more stubborn than any other animal she'd ever encountered—including her own father. And now Brendan knew about him! In two hour—tops—the entire family would know, and she'd never hear the end of it. Damn it! She was going to strangle Drake. Closing her eyes, she sucked in a couple of deep breaths. The roundabout way she'd taken home certainly hadn't done anything to settle her temper. First the damn spook chasing Garth had showed up and then she'd had to deal with Drake. When the door opened again then closed, Melody spun around to glare at her brother as he walked into her bedroom while jerking his jeans up to his waist. Poking her finger into his chest, she began, "Brendan, if you tell—"

She never got the chance to finish her threat.

"Shut up, get some clothes on, and come to the kitchen," he growled. Spinning on his heel, he left her staring at the empty doorway.

Struggling into the robe she'd picked up from her porch where she'd discarded it earlier and carried into the house with her, she followed him toward the back of the cabin. "What the hell do you think you're doing, ordering me around as if I'm one of your employees—in my own house?" she snarled when she caught up to him. "Well, I'm not, and you're not..."

After glancing out the kitchen window, he stood next to the table. "Christ, Melody, will you just shut up and listen?"

When he had her undivided attention, he continued after he jerked his tee shirt over his head, "You're being watched. Your wolf told me he saw a man on the hill above your cabin watching you. I swung up there before I came back to the house. The wolf is right. There's a guy up there in camouflage with a pair of high-tech binoculars."

For a moment Melody simply stared at her brother. Then, after a long, low growl, she spun around and headed for the back door. "That fucking CIA asshole. Wait until I get my hands and teeth on him." She glared back over her shoulder. "And Drake is *not* my wolf."

Her brother grabbed the back of her robe before she could leave the kitchen. "Damn it, Melody. Leave the CIA guy be. As long as he's here, he's not chasing Garth. Eileen's pregnant."

That halted Melody in her tracks, and she turned. "Garth is going to be a daddy? I'm going to be an aunt again?" She knew she was now grinning like an idiot, but she didn't care. Another cub to add to the clan was wonderful news. "When is she due?"

"Not for another six months or so, but the last thing we need is Garth dragging her off into the wilds of Canada. Belle filled you in on what Eileen's life was like all those years Garth didn't know where she was. She's finally relaxed and happy with Belle and Alex's pack, and the family would like to keep it that way. Dad's contact in the CIA is completely off his disability leave and back to work. He should be able to recall this guy chasing Garth in a week or so. Can you keep him tied up that long?"

Crossing her arms over her chest, Melody nodded at her brother. "I can keep him busy."

Brendan nodded back then grinned. "You can always ask your boyfriend for help."

The fist she buried in his stomach knocked the breath from his lungs.

When he finally stopped choking, he gasped, "Shit,

Melody. I was only kidding. Why did you have to punch me so hard?"

"Well, I'm sick and tired of your kidding. That wolf is almost as much a pain-in-the-ass as you are. The sooner he leaves me alone, the better."

Hands fisted on her hips, Melody watched as her brother shook his head and said, "I don't think this particular wolf will give up on you now that he's made up his mind. You may have to disappear for a while. After we get everything with Garth settled, why don't you go visit Dad and Moira. Your wolf won't be able to follow you to New York."

"He's not *my* wolf, Brendan, so don't make his obsession into anything more than it is. He'll leave sooner or later. I'm more stubborn than he is."

Her brother chuckled. "Too bad he's not human. You could have him arrested for stalking."

Shoving him out of the way, Melody grabbed the tea kettle and filled it with water. "Go home, Brendan, before I rip out some of that thick, silver hair you love so much. You don't want to have to explain bald spots to all those women who fawn over you."

With another chuckle, he dropped onto a kitchen chair and pulled on his boots. "They'd fawn over me even more wanting to know how I got injured."

After placing the filled kettle on the stove, Melody turned back to her brother. "One day you're going to find a woman who doesn't think you're the greatest thing since sliced bread, and I hope I'm there to see it. Do you want some tea before you leave?"

A wide grin splitting his face, Brendan rose to his feet. "No thanks. I have to get back to Garth and let him know what's going on here."

"You'll be staying with Garth and Eileen?"

He shook his head. "In the bed and breakfast Belle's pack owns for a day or two. Garth's cabin is on the side of a mountain in the middle of fucking nowhere, and he's got a pair of old wolves living under the front porch who insist on growling at me."

When Melody stopped laughing, she grinned then said, "Good for them. They recognize a scoundrel when they see one."

Brendan grinned back. "Just like your Drake recognizes his mate when he sees her?" He quickly sidestepped then pulled her into a tight hug before she could smack him. "Take care, Mel. Watch out for that CIA guy. Garth said he's very, very good, and that makes him entirely too dangerous. Call if you need me, and I'll come back. If we have to get rid of this guy, we will. I can make sure his body is never found."

Melody hugged him back. "That will be the last resort. We'd have Feds crawling all over town and into everybody's business. The Pack here is small, but it still doesn't want to call attention to itself."

Brendan stepped back and stared at her. "You haven't had any trouble from any of them, have you, because you refused to join?"

Melody smiled and shook her head. "The Pack here in Beacon Falls is very loosely organized. I don't think any *Were* has ever 'officially' joined. Sheriff Dan Rivers is the Alpha, and his wife Shirley is a doll. They've taken it upon themselves to adopt every *Were* in the vicinity. Cail Brown is the town doctor, and his wife Julie helps Shirley in the café. Those four are the Pack's core. There are maybe three or four dozen or so other permanent *Were* residents in the town and the surrounding countryside and forest. All of them come and go as they please, and as long as they don't bring attention to themselves, Dan leaves them alone."

Her brother nodded. "Belle's Alex runs a much tighter ship. He and his Betas keep track of everything going on. Of course, they've got over a hundred members in their Pack."

The kettle began to whistle.

"Are you sure you don't want some tea?" Melody asked again as she lifted the kettle and turned off the burner. After pouring the hot water into a cup, she set it in the sink then got a tea bag from a nearby canister.

Her brother shook his head. "No, now that I've filled you in on everything, I need to get back. I will probably swing over by Kearnan's, though. Dad and Moira have decided to visit everybody, and Belle's place is centrally located, so to speak." He grinned. "So I'm also delivering an order to make sure you have yourself at Belle's in two weeks, or you'll face Dad's wrath."

"What if the CIA asshole isn't gone?"

"He will be. Dad's friend at the CIA promised he'd be gone in a week tops so make sure you're at Belle's. You haven't met Moira or our new sisters yet, and Dad wants to give Belle's and Kearnan's mates the once-over."

After blowing on her hot tea, Melody cocked an eyebrow. "Not Eileen?"

Her brother grinned back. "He approved of Eileen a long time ago, and since Kearnan and Serena have a daughter, he's going to love Kearnan's mate on sight. He'll probably give Alex a hard time though."

Melody shook her head. Belle's new mate was going to be in for a rough time. "Poor Alex, mating Dad's little girl. I hope he's up to the meeting. You know what Dad can be like."

Brendan grinned even more widely. "Why don't you bring your wolf with you? I bet Dad likes him."

Choking mid gulp, Melody dropped her cup on the table and sprang for her brother.

He was already sprinting out of the kitchen, across the living room, and out the front door.

Melody was on his heels.

When she burst through the door and leaped off the porch, he wrapped his arms around her in a tight hug. "Remember, we're being watched."

Wrapping her arms around his ribs, she squeezed until he grunted.

"Not so damn hard!"

"You deserve it. If we weren't being watched, I'd bite you, but that asshole up there would definitely get the wrong message."

Loosening Melody's hold, Brendan stepped back. "Like I said, be careful. This guy is a pro, and he's looking for werewolves. That makes him more dangerous than anyone any of us have encountered. Don't take any chances. I'm going to swing around by the sheriff's office and fill him in while our friend is here watching you. Do something suspicious to keep him here a while, okay?"

Melody frowned. "What the hell do I ever do that's suspicious? You want me to stand out here and howl at the sun or something?"

Chuckling, Brendan hugged her once more then stepped back off the porch. "Remember, Dad expects to see all of us at Belle's."

Nodding, Melody waved as her brother slid into his SUV. She remained standing in the sun until he disappeared into the trees. Then she returned to the porch and checked to see if the flowering baskets hanging from the eaves needed to be watered. After that, she stepped back into her cabin, shaking her head as she did so. Do something suspicious to keep the spook on the hill interested? Just what the hell was she supposed to do? Build a bomb?

Closing the front door firmly behind her, she locked it and set the alarm though she doubted very much that Nick Price would try to enter while she was home. He didn't impress her as being that stupid, even if he probably thought he could overpower her.

Melody smiled at that thought. She'd love to see him try.

Leaving her living room curtains open—closing them would be too suspicious—she walked into the kitchen, cleaned up the spilled tea, and made sure the back door was also locked. Then she made herself another cup of tea. As she swallowed, she shook her head. Damn but she and Brendan had been lucky. If they'd approached her cabin from the front instead of the back and shifted into human form there, Nick Price, CIA agent, wouldn't have to go chasing after Garth. He'd have been down that hill after *them*. Granted, together they'd have made short work of him, but, as she'd told Brendan earlier, that would have brought more federal agents to town looking for him. Not only would the *Weres* of Beacon Falls have been unhappy, there were humans here who didn't want any Feds poking around either.

Finishing her tea, Melody set the cup in the sink and sauntered into the bedroom. She needed to get a shower then get into town. No matter what Brendan said or wanted, she had a business to run. Glancing once at the drapes pushed back to either side of the window, Melody considered closing them. Then she smiled.

Nick Price was watching her? Well, maybe she should give him something worthwhile to watch. Opening the sash on her robe, she slid it off her shoulders and let it puddle around her feet. Raising her arms, she pushed herself up onto her tiptoes and arched her back. After settling back onto her feet, she smiled, made sure she faced the window directly, and cupped her breasts. If Mr. Nick fucking Price of the fucking CIA wanted to watch her, she'd give him a show worth watching.

Falling back onto her bed, she spread her legs and slid her hands down over her stomach.

Chapter Five

ഗ

"Who the hell was that?" Nick muttered to himself as he stepped to the left and refocused his binoculars to watch the powerful four-by-four disappear down the road into the forest, the dust billowing behind it.

For the last four hours, Nick had been on the hill above Melody Gray's house. Two vehicles had been parked next to the cabin when he'd arrived, and he'd been patiently waiting to see who her guest was. As time went on and he'd seen no movement in the cabin, he'd considered going down to take a closer look. Then Melody had walked naked into her bedroom followed by the gray-haired guy as he was pulling up his pants.

As Melody and her guest disappeared from his line of sight again, Nick lowered his binoculars and shook his head. They must have had one hell of a fuck-fest in the kitchen. Then she'd chased him across the living room and out of the cabin before hugging him goodbye.

An irritated blue jay on the branch above Nick squawked then dropped a twig on his head.

"Fucking birds," he grumbled as he shifted back to his right and slipped a little on the soft loam. "I can't wait to feel cement under my feet again. Fuck Sorescu and this assignment. He's a fucking idiot who needs his fucking head examined. Werewolves my fucking ass."

A branch snapped behind him and he whirled, the memory of the wolf he'd seen the night before leaping into his mind. The flash of a white tail had him relaxing immediately. A deer. Nothing to be worried about there.

For a few seconds, he stared into the woods where the

deer had disappeared then shook his head. "Quit bitching, Price," he growled to himself. "You've been up to your armpits in swamp water filled with poisonous snakes and spitting the grit from a sandstorm out of your mouth while a sniper was taking pot shots at you. All things considered, this is a cake job. All you have to do is find out what Gray really knows then you can move on. Hurley went north. His trail will turn up."

Turning back around, he refocused his binoculars to look through the window of Melody's bedroom—and almost dropped them. She was spread-eagled on the bed finger-fucking herself. His high-tech binoculars were so sensitive, he could see the drops of moisture on the lips of her cunt.

Swallowing, Nick let the binoculars drop and hang against his chest by the strap. Christ, didn't that guy who'd been with her for the last four hours satisfy her? Was that why she chased him across the living room? She was still horny? What was she, a nymphomaniac?

Glancing up between the dark, green pine branches at the cloudless blue sky, Nick swore to himself and rose to his feet. He should head back down the mountain to his hotel, pack everything up and take off after Hurley. That's what he should do. The hell with the gut feeling that kept telling him Melody Gray knew more about his quarry than she was letting on. His gut was telling him something else now—this Gray woman was more trouble than he wanted and she would fuck his life up even more than Sorescu had. The smart thing to do was get the hell away while the getting was good.

Propping his hands on his hips, Nick continued to stare at the sky. Run from a woman? Shit, no man had ever scared him off a job, not even that torturer in Algeria. And the only woman he was afraid of in any way was the aunt who raised him. A brief smile twitched at the corners of his mouth. His Aunt Jasmine was a woman nobody fucked with. She'd have voodoo curses flying right and left.

A small chuckled erupted from his throat and Nick shook

his head. Aunt Jasmine would be putting curses on him if he didn't finish what he started here. If he thought Melody Gray knew something, then he'd better make damn sure he found out what it was. His Aunt Jasmine, even without her supposed voodoo, could mess up his life a hell of a lot more than Melody Gray.

Nick snorted. Voodoo, ha! Voodoo was about as real as werewolves. But his Aunt Jasmine believed in it, and she was the most important person in his life. She'd raised him after his parents had been killed in that traffic accident. She'd made sure he understood both sides of his heritage, the African-American and the British, even though many of her friends had disapproved of his "white education". Jasmine hadn't cared what they thought. Nick's mother hadn't cared that the man she loved was white. To her, the inside of a person was what mattered, and his Aunt Jasmine had made sure Nick learned that.

Nick continued to smile at his memories. Aunt Jasmine had taken on an eleven-year-old without a second thought and brought joy back into his life. She'd been aunt, mother and sister all rolled into one and had supported him in all his endeavors. She'd been so proud when he'd graduated from college, then hadn't so much as blinked when he'd told her he wanted to join the CIA even though she didn't trust the agency to "take care of her boy". No, she'd supported him one hundred percent.

Now, just one disappointed look in her eyes or one sad word in her smoky voice would have his heart aching. She'd taught him to finish what he started and he wasn't about to disappoint her for the world. So if she wanted to believe in voodoo, that was all right with Nick. As frustrating as Melody Gray would probably become, he was going to stay here until he figured out exactly what she was hiding.

Lifting the binoculars, he refocused them on Melody—and immediately spat out a curse. One of her hands cupped her breast while the thumb flicked her nipple, and the fingers of her other hand were dancing in her cunt and around her clit. He looked up at the sky once more as a bead of sweat rolled down the side of his face. He should just leave, but instead he lowered his gaze and raised the binoculars. For the life of him, he couldn't bring himself to look away.

As he watched Melody arch her back and pump her hips against her hand, his cock twitched and thickened.

Closing his eyes, Nick focused his will to bring his body back under control. Over the years, he'd dispassionately observed more than one sexual act while staking out suspects, many far more erotic—or kinky—than that of a woman masturbating. Never once had his body reacted to anything he'd seen. Now his cock was stretched out against his leg, getting harder by the second. What the fuck was it about this particular woman that shot his control to hell?

When his body refused to subjugate itself to his will, Nick opened his eyes. Gritting his teeth, he ignored his now throbbing cock. No woman was going to make him lose his self-control—not even if he had to live with this fucking hard-on all day.

Surrounded by the scent of her arousal, Melody moaned and sighed while her fingers danced with her clit. She hadn't meant to become so worked up, had planned simply to play with herself for a while so her watcher concentrated on her rather than following Brendan. But the thought of Nick Price watching and the memory of how…*hard*…his torso had looked in that tight tee shirt he'd been wearing when he'd first walked into her office had quickly derailed her plan. Instead, she fantasized that he was here now, the shirt gone and his well-defined, coffee-colored muscles covered with slick sweat while his dark, jerking cock stabbed the air. And he was wearing the same superior smile he'd had on his face in her office yesterday.

As she rubbed her clit, Melody shivered. Son of a bitch, but Price had a cocky attitude, one she'd love to slap off his face. But then, as her clit tightened and began to throb, she slipped deeper into her fantasy.

Nick Price slid his rough hand up the inside of her thigh and buried a couple fingers into her slippery cunt.

"Oh gods," Melody moaned as she arched against his hand. "Please…"

"You like that? Want more?" he asked while he pumped his fingers in and out.

"Yes, oh, yes!" Moaning, she screwed herself down.

"Fuck but you're wet." Pulling his hand away, he settled between her legs and kneed her thighs wider apart. "Spread those legs for me, baby."

As he settled his hips against hers and slid his cock up and down against her clit, Melody's moans became frustrated groans. "Stop playing, damn it! I need your cock inside me, now!"

He lowered his head and sucked on her tingling nipple. Then he raised his face and looked into her eyes. "Whatever you say, baby." One hard thrust had his cock buried in her cunt.

Melody howled with joy.

He pulled back and thrust again, burying himself even deeper. Again he pulled out, again he thrust deeply.

Melody wrapped her legs around his waist and her internal muscles sucked his cock as deeply inside of her as they could.

His rhythm increased and she matched it—thrust for thrust, twist for twist.

Panting, she dug her fingers into the smooth, dark skin of his ass and tried to pull him deeper.

"Yeah, baby. That's it. Grab my ass. Squeeze it."

Lost in her fantasy, Melody moaned as she pinched her nipple. Thigh and abdominal muscles shuddering, she arched her back and rubbed her clit harder. As the bed rocked beneath her, she exploded into orgasm.

Up on the hill, more sweat rolled down Nick's forehead as he watched Melody thrash her head from side to side and gyrate her hips wildly. One moment she had her heels braced down against the mattress, the next she was raising them into the air. She spread her legs wider then closed them against her whirling fingers. All the while, her hips twisted and turned as she ground them against her hand.

Nick's heart pounded and his cock throbbed in unison inside his tight jeans. Gritting his teeth, he fought the urge to free his erection and pump himself to fulfillment. Sex was never part of a job he did, and he wasn't about to change now, even if it was with himself.

Down in the bedroom, Melody suddenly stopped moving as her body stiffened. Only the fingers on her clit moved until, finally, her entire body arched off the bed.

Even up on the hill, Nick heard her scream of ecstasy.

At that exact moment, fire erupted from Nick's balls, and hot, sticky cum spurted into his too-tight jeans as he staggered for balance. Dropping the binoculars against his chest, he reached out with his left hand and braced it against a nearby sapling to keep from falling to his knees. Christ! He hadn't even touched himself and his knees were shaking so badly they could barely support him. He didn't have to look down to know a large wet spot was staining the left leg of his jeans. Shaking his head, he stared down at the cabin. What kind of woman was this Melody Gray? No one had ever affected him like this before.

Still breathing heavily, Melody swung her legs over the side of the bed and sat up. Once her heart stopped racing, she pushed herself to her feet only to flop down on the bed when her knees wobbled and her legs wouldn't support her. Pushing her hair back over her forehead, she stared at herself in the dresser mirror. A bead of sweat rolled down her forehead onto her cheek. Her face was flushed as were her breasts. Both were still tingling, and her nipples were distended farther than she'd ever seen them. Spasms of heat were still stabbing her cunt. By all the gods, she'd never had an orgasm like that one before, neither alone nor with someone else!

Shaking her head, she took a couple of deep breaths and pushed herself to her feet. She still wobbled, but this time remained standing. After a few more deep breaths, she staggered to her shower. Work, she had to get to work. Maybe then she could get her mind on more serious matters, like how she was going to keep Nick Price from picking up her brother's trail. Her snort erupted around her small bathroom. If he was half as good in reality as he was in her fantasy, she just might handcuff him to her bed for a few weeks. She could think of more than a few ways to keep him busy—and exhausted.

As she turned on the water for her shower, she snorted a second time. What was she thinking? Keep Price in her house? Like hell. She didn't care how good he was in bed. Nick Price was a dangerous man, and she was going to keep him at arm's length. Who cared how good fantasy sex was anyway?

Chapter Six

ഇ

As Melody entered the outer office of her agency, she didn't need to read the sign John held up that said, "We've been bugged" to know that Nick Price had been there while the building had been empty. His scent permeated not only the outer office but also hers. Following Price's spoor from place to place, she quickly found the four electronic devices he'd scattered in various locations in the two offices.

What should we do?

Melody blinked and shook her head. Most unrelated werewolves rarely communicated mind-to-mind while in their human forms. For some reason it was harder—something to do with the fact that they could speak as humans and their brains wanted to use their vocal cords, according to werewolf scientists who'd studied the matter. Still it was a good way to "talk" privately with someone.

Staring at John, she focused her thoughts and concentrated. *Nothing. If we destroy or disable them, he'll know we found them. At this point, he thinks we're a couple of hick private dicks. I don't want him thinking any differently. We need to keep him occupied until my father's contact gets him recalled to Washington.*

John grinned at her. *You're the boss.*

Melody nodded. *Okay then, normal conversation, with some local gossip to keep Price entertained.* "Anything new come in, John?" she asked as she made her way back into her office.

She left the door open. Once Nick Price got tired of listening to the town's scuttlebutt she and John were going to talk about for the next hour or so, he'd probably get so bored he'd come stomping into the office with some flimsy excuse about an inconsistency in the file on Jake Fields just to see what they were doing. Melody grinned. Pissing off a pain-in-the-ass CIA spook when he thought she didn't know what he was doing could be fun.

John picked up a stack of files. "Nothing new. Just as well, we have a ton of paperwork to catch up on."

Melody wrinkled her nose. Crap, but that was a big stack of files. Had they really gotten that far behind? Considering how far back in the sticks they were, she was often amazed at how much business she had. "I hate paperwork."

John's chuckle rippled around her. "Too bad. It has to be done. I keep telling you to hire a secretary. There's a lot more work out here in the boondocks for private investigators than I ever figured. I'm supposed to be semi-retired, you know."

Melody snorted. "You? Retire? All seven hells will freeze over first." After a quick wink to her coworker, she changed the subject. Time to start entertaining Price. "How's Penny? Is she feeling better today?"

Penny was John's neighbor's pregnant Irish Setter, but Price didn't know that.

John caught on right away. "She's doing okay, I guess. Pretty snappish toward me. The only one she'll let near her now is Frank."

"Penny is his, you know. I don't know why you can't leave her alone, and I don't know why your Martha puts up with you mooning after Penny. She'd as soon clobber you with a frying pan as share you."

John chuckled. "It's all that red hair Penny has. Have you ever seen anything so soft and silky in all your life?"

"You and red hair. It's going to get you into trouble big-time one of these days, and Martha will send you packing with your tail between your legs."

"Now, Melody, you know my Martha loves me. She couldn't live without me."

Biting the insides of her cheek to keep from laughing, Melody took a deep breath then said, "You just keep telling yourself that, John. Don't say I didn't warn you. How are the Wallace twins, by the way?"

"Those two? Getting into trouble like always. Everybody thought the chicken pox would slow them down, but they snuck out of their room, grabbed their bikes, and tried to pedal down that steep gully behind their house. They ended up crashing through old lady Deigen's fence and tearing down her clean laundry."

Melody chuckled. "Old lady Deigen, huh? Those boys are in big trouble."

"Yep," John said as he pulled his pipe out of a drawer and knocked the bowl against his palm. "She grabbed each one by an ear and dragged them off to the sheriff's office. Folks said the look on their mother's face when she got those boys home woulda scared the shit out of an army ranger," he finished as he thumbed tobacco down into his pipe. Lighting a match, he clamped the stem between his lips and puffed.

Melody shook her head. "I thought you told Martha you gave up smoking that smelly thing? You'll be sorry when she finds out you haven't."

Shaking out the match, he grinned then said, "But she won't find out as long as you don't tell her."

The door slammed open before Melody could reply, and she had to take a firm hold of herself so she didn't laugh in Nick Price's face. Looked like he couldn't take local gossip for more than a few minutes.

"Morning, Mr. Price, what can we do for you?" Melody asked as she pulled her gaze from his muscular torso—damn but he was built—and looked into his face. Unlike the previous day when she'd first met Nick, Melody was no longer exhausted. She was completely awake now with her senses totally alert. Her gaze traveled up over his strong, black chin and mobile lips, which were drawn into a tight line, looked into his chocolaty-brown eyes, and almost crumpled to the floor as her werewolf soul roared to full life.

Mine! He is mine, mine, mine! Mate! My mate! He is my mate!

Gasping for breath, Melody doubled over and grabbed the edge of John's desk to keep from falling—or leaping into Price's arms.

"Melody!" John yelped as he leaped to her side. "What's wrong? Are you okay?" He placed one hand in the small of her back and gripped her shoulder with the other.

"I…I…" With his help, she pushed herself upright. Knuckles whitening as she clutched the edge of the desk, she fought to control the werewolf raging inside of her—the werewolf that wanted to launch itself onto Price's hard body.

Momentarily taken aback by Melody's unexpected action, Nick simply stared at her as she practically doubled over, idly wondering if her explosive masturbation from earlier this morning could have something to do with it. When her partner jumped to her side, though, he frowned. Maybe she *was* sick. "Can I get you anything? Some water? Should I call a doctor or 9-1-1 or something?"

When she turned her face toward him and glared at him with wild, gold-flecked eyes, Nick stepped back. Christ, but that was one weird look. Then he frowned. Yesterday, her eyes had been a clear, deep blue, he was absolutely sure of it. Where did those gold flecks come from? What the hell was going on?

Dropping her head so that her long, white-blonde hair fell forward and covered her face, she sucked in a deep breath then let it out again. "No…Mr. Price," she choked out. "That…won't be necessary. I'm fine."

Nick leaned closer. He had to get another look at her eyes. "You don't look fine. Does your side hurt? You might have appendicitis."

She shook her head, took another deep breath, and straightened. "I can assure you, Mr. Price, I do not have appendicitis." The stare in her blue eyes was both a challenge and a warning.

Nick stepped back again. Challenge? Warning? What the hell was going on? Questions and suspicions rolling around in his mind, Nick stared back.

Grimacing, she dropped her gaze and took another deep breath. The expression on her face went completely blank and the look in her eyes became completely shuttered. She looked him in the eye again. "What can we do for you, Mr. Price?"

Searching for any sign of weakness that he could exploit, Nick locked gazes with her. "I have a couple questions about the file you gave me."

Her gaze never left his. "Talk to John. It was his case." Spinning on her heel, she strode into her office and closed the door firmly behind her.

"What do you want to know?" her partner asked. "I thought everything I put in there was pretty cut and dried."

Nick pulled his stare away from her door and turned his attention to John Stevens. While he listened to what Gray's partner had to say with half of his mind, the other half was locked on Melody Gray's actions. That look of shock and surprise in her eyes had been real. What had caused it? She had to be hiding something about Hurley she wasn't telling him. He was sure of it now.

In her office, Melody collapsed into her chair and stared at the wall. Her soul was railing against her, but she had herself firmly under control now. Of all her siblings, her will was the strongest. She'd been the first to accomplish the shift from wolf form to human, the first of her brothers and sister to master and hold it as long as she wanted. Her father had not been in favor of her starting her own detective agency so far from his protection, but she'd held her ground, out-shouted and out-growled him, and done as she'd pleased. Up until this day, her life had been wonderful.

Now, however, one man had turned her life completely upside down.

A tear rolled down her cheek, and she fingered it away.

Mate Nick Price? A human? The freaking CIA spook who was after her brother was her mate, was the other half of her soul? What the hell was going on? This wasn't supposed to happen! Oh, she'd known that one day sometime—preferably years from now—she'd encounter the man who was supposed to be her mate. But today? A human? She wasn't ready. What had she ever done to deserve this fate?

As another tear rolled down her cheek, Melody sniffed then growled. Nick Price was the man who wanted to lock her brother away for the rest of his life! How could he be her mate?

Chapter Seven

ℌ

"I still say you should go home," John said as he held the door open to Big Kate's Gentlemen's Saloon and Dance Hall, the favored bar and restaurant of many of the town's inhabitants. "You've had quite a shock."

"And what would I do there?" Melody asked as she stomped into the bar. "Sit and stare at the walls? Go for a run? If I did that, Drake would show up, then I'd have to deal with another male I don't want. No thanks. I want a beer—a couple of beers." Plopping herself down onto a stool at the end of the bar, she caught the bartender's attention, held up two fingers, and glanced at her partner. "You want a beer too, right?"

The burly bartender sauntered down to their end of the bar holding two sweating, long-necked, brown bottles in his hand.

As soon as he set one in front of her, Melody grabbed it, upended it, and chugged the icy beer. Thunking the empty down, she said, "Give me another one."

"Guess you don't want a glass," the bartender muttered as he quirked an eyebrow at John.

Melody's partner shrugged.

"Rough day at work?" the big man asked as he set another beer in front of Melody.

"I don't want to talk about it, Bart," she answered as she pulled the icy bottle closer. This time, though, she simply sipped her beer. Swiveling her seat, she watched her partner and the bartender out of the corner of her eye while she pretended to stare at the two men shooting pool.

Again the bartender cocked an eyebrow at John.

John shook his head then said, "Martha's meeting me for supper."

"You want a table in the dining room?"

John glanced at Melody. "We'd rather have a booth here in the bar, Bart."

"Sure thing. The one in the corner okay?"

Melody's partner cocked his foot on the brass railing, rested an arm on the bar, and nodded. "That'll do just fine." He lifted his beer and took a long, slow swig. "Been fishing lately?"

Wiping the already clean bar with a white towel, Bart shook his head. "Nope. Haven't had the time. Been thinking about going Sunday, though. Interested in tagging along?"

Ignoring the conversation at her side now that it wasn't about her—Bart and John could talk fishing for hours on end—Melody slid off her stool and sauntered toward the pool table. Once there, she propped one hip on the stool at the end of the bar and continued to sip her beer as she forced herself to try to concentrate on the game. The werewolf in her soul wouldn't allow her any peace.

My mate! Go now. Mate him. Now!

She gulped more beer. Damn it, but the animal half of her was tenacious. Once her wolf half set its mind on something, it was like a dog worrying a bone.

The internal snarl at comparing a wolf to a dog, an animal who'd given up freedom and chained itself to humans, caused Melody's lips to twitch, but her smile didn't last long. After another gulp of beer, she raked her hair back off her forehead. Damn it! She wasn't ready to be mated, was she? And why a human, especially one as arrogant as Nick Price? She didn't even like him. Did she?

A picture of Nick the first time he'd walked into her office popped into her mind—the dark handsome face below a smoothly shaved head, camo pants, and a tight, black tee shirt over a broad chest and well-developed biceps. And even though his camouflage pants had been loose, his ass had looked pretty damn good in them when he'd walked out of her office.

The crack of one ball hitting another and masculine laughter wrenched her from her musings. Blinking, she found herself staring into the local feed store owner's smiling face.

"How about a game, Melody? Ben here isn't any kind of challenge. He smashed his finger pulling spark plugs from that old truck of his."

Concentrating on the comforting aroma of good food wafting from the kitchen behind the bar, the spicy odor of the beer she carried, and the familiar scents of the bar's patrons, Melody began to relax. Shoving the nagging werewolf part of her into a small compartment in her mind, she slammed the door shut on her thoughts of Nick, turned to the tall man who'd addressed her and smiled. "Sure, Dan. I'd like that." *It will give me something else to think about.* "You rack 'em. I'll break." Grabbing a pool stick, she twirled it around her fingers a couple of times as she made her way to the other end of the pool table, rolling her neck and shoulders to work out the kinks. Bending over the edge of the table, she shot the cue ball into the colorful triangle of balls at the other end of the table. Stripes and solids rolled in all directions when the white ball smacked into them.

None fell into a pocket.

Dan grinned. "Your game's off, Melody. Maybe I'll beat you tonight."

Melody shook her head. "Not a chance, Dan. I'm just feeling sorry for you and decided to give you a head start."

As masculine laughter echoed around the bar, Melody began to relax. Everyone here was a friend.

Shifting to the other side of the table after Dan successfully dropped the two and five balls into pockets but missed with the six, Melody grinned. "Stripes for me. Are you ready to be schooled now, Dan?"

He shook his head ruefully. "Do your worst, Mel."

Melody grinned wider. "I plan to do my best." A quick snap of her wrist and the ten ball rolled into the corner pocket quickly followed by the thirteen and the nine.

"Looks like you're in trouble, Dan," Ben said from his seat at the bar when Melody sank the eleven ball. "She's hot tonight."

Just as Melody was about to run the table and hit the eight ball into a side pocket, an enticing scent wafted across the room and wrapped itself around her.

Her werewolf soul shoved that door in her mind wide open. *Mine! Mine! Mine!*

She hit the ball off center. It slammed into the four ball and knocked it into a side pocket.

"Damn!" Straightening, she wrestled for control while doing her best to ignore the man who'd just settled onto a stool at the bar. Why did Nick Price have to show up just when she'd managed to get him locked away in a tiny corner of her mind where he couldn't bother her?

Dan whooped at her miss. "Thanks, Mel." Lining up his shot, he knocked another one of his balls into a pocket.

Turning her back to Nick, Melody glared off into space as she kept the wolf inside of her firmly under control. She was not a bitch in heat to shake her tail at her mate to make him chase her.

She stiffened even more as her eyes widened. Her mate? The knuckles of the hand wrapped around her pool stick whitened. *Her mate?* She'd called him that? Even to herself?

"Melody!"

She wrenched her attention back to the pool table. "What!"

"Stop woolgathering, girl! Dan missed his shot. It's your turn," Ben yelled.

After a slight, she hoped unnoticed, shudder, Melody

examined the pool table then shook her head at the easy shot she had. All she had to do was tap the cue ball and the twelve would drop into the left-side pocket. Still, she took her time lining up the shot. Missing would be too embarrassing.

While she concentrated, she ignored the noise and scents of other patrons in the bar—until someone stopped directly behind her.

"Here, honey, let me help you with that." Leaning over her back, he placed his hands over hers on the stick.

Frustration directed at the entire male sex roared to life. Not another one! "Kenny, get off me before I make you sorry you're alive," she snarled. Warm breath rolled down both sides of her neck as he chuckled then whispered in her ear, "Come on now, Melody, honey. You know you can't resist me. Besides, you're mine. No other *Were* around here is good enough for you." He rubbed his crotch against her ass. "Let's go somewhere we can be alone."

"Like hell." Shifting her hips to the side, Melody yanked the pool stick backward. When she slammed it into Kenny's balls, he screamed, jerked his hands off hers to cover his crotch and doubled over in pain. As his head came down, Melody lifted the stick so it solidly connected with his chin. Lifting one hand from his crotch to grab his chin, he howled again and fell to his knees.

Whirling, the pool stick clenched in her hands, Melody snarled, "I warned you to leave me alone, Kenny."

"You…fucking…bitch! Get you…for this!" Kenny gasped as he struggled to regain his feet.

As his three leather- and chain-clad friends converged on Melody, the sound of a shotgun being pumped drowned out Kenny's gasping curses.

"What seems to be the problem here?" asked a new voice.

Stepping back away from the four men before her, Melody stared at the sheriff. "Kenny assaulted me and I defended myself."

The tall man pushed his hat back on his head and looked to Dan and Ben.

Both shrugged.

"He flopped himself down over her while she was taking her shot," Ben said. "Then he rubbed himself up against her. I'd a' done the same thing Melody did."

Nodding, the sheriff stared at Kenny. "You've been warned to leave Melody alone. She has no interest in you, Kenny. How stupid are you?"

The young, blond-haired man struggled to his feet. "I want her! Nobody else around here is strong enough to ma—"

Bart pumped the shotgun again as the sheriff stepped forward and grabbed Kenny by the lapels of his leather jacket. His tirade stopped abruptly. "Shut up, Kenny, and get out of here before I lock you up for disturbing the peace."

Snarling a curse, the young man pushed himself out of the sheriff's grasp. Glancing over at Melody, he growled, "You'll regret this, bitch."

The sheriff grabbed him by the arm and shoved him toward the door. "Go now before I add making threats of bodily harm to the list."

Still snarling and followed by his sneering cronies, Kenny stumbled down the length of the bar and out through the swinging doors.

Shaking his head, the sheriff nodded to Bart. "You can put your shotgun away now—and it better not be loaded!" He turned to Melody. "You okay?"

Melody nodded. "I'm fine."

"Kenny's not going to take this public rejection quietly, Melody. You watch yourself and call me if there's any trouble," the sheriff added quietly.

Raking her hair back, Melody nodded. "I can handle Kenny. You don't have to worry about me."

"It's Kenny I'm worried about," the sheriff answered with

a grin. "I don't want to be the one explaining to his mama if you manage to geld him the next time."

The tension that had been enveloping Melody loosened its grip at the sheriff's comment. Everyone in town constantly shook their heads at Kenny's attempts to court Melody ever since she'd first arrived four years ago, even though she'd made it plain on more than one occasion that she wasn't interested. Up until today, her rejections had been relatively gentle.

Melody sighed. Maybe she had gone overboard today, but her emotions had been on a roller coaster ride ever since she'd looked into Nick Price's eyes earlier that day. In this state, no werewolf could completely control her reactions.

Unfortunately, most of the town didn't know she and Kenny were werewolves.

"Are you sure you're okay, Melody? You look a bit peaked."

Melody smiled a weak smile. "I'm fine, Sheriff, really."

The sheriff glanced at John.

He nodded slightly.

Melody gritted her teeth. If only there weren't any humans here. She'd give her werewolf brethren—John, Bart and the sheriff—an earful, and maybe a few well-placed nips. She didn't need them acting as if they were her fathers—again. Honestly, if she didn't know better, she'd swear her father had them keeping tabs on her.

That suspicious thought whirling around in her mind, she glared at them and began, "Listen, you guys, did my dad ever…"

She was interrupted by another voice that caused the werewolf in her to rumble with joy.

"Feel like another game of pool, Ms. Gray?" Standing on the other side of the table, Nick Price chalked the end of a pool cue. "I'll break."

Chapter Eight

ꟿ

Before she could answer, Nick turned, racked the balls, spotted the cue ball and slammed his stick into it. As the crack of ball hitting ball reverberated around the room, solid and striped spheres rolled and ricocheted around the pool table and off its sides.

Not a single ball fell into a pocket.

For a moment she stared at the table. Then, sighing mentally, she gave in to the wolf inside her. What could a game of pool hurt? "You sure you know how to play this game?" she asked as she leaned over the table and knocked a striped ball into a corner pocket.

"You knock the balls into the holes," Nick answered. "I can handle that."

Her smile was a bit superior as she sank another shot. "We'll see."

Turning his back on her, Nick sauntered over to the bar, dropped a ten dollar bill, and held up two fingers.

"She'll kick your ass, you know," the bartender said as he handed Nick the beers.

Grunting in acknowledgment, Nick turned away and rolled the bartender's comment around his mind. On the surface, he could have been commenting on Melody's obvious mastery of pool. On the other hand, the bartender could be referring to something else. Nick had arrived in the bar before her altercation with the young punk named Kenny. She'd twirled the pool stick in her hands more than once, undoubtedly unconsciously. Judging by her skill, she'd either been a baton twirler in high school or she'd had martial arts training. Somehow, Nick couldn't imagine Melody Gray as the type who twirled batons. His intuition had been proved correct when she disabled Kenny with two blows of the stick. It had been nicely done, without any extra motion.

Nick was impressed.

Placing Melody's beer on a table, he sipped his and watched her make her way around the table as she knocked ball after ball into the pockets. Stopping in front of him, she bent over the table to make a somewhat difficult shot.

Nick allowed his gaze to drift up the length of her long legs as he swigged more beer. At first, he'd thought of her as too tall and too skinny for his taste, but the way her tight jeans hugged her ass was nice, very nice.

"You keep staring at Melody's ass like that and you'll wear a hole in her jeans, CIA man," the bartender said in a voice loud enough to carry just as Melody was about to shoot.

As Nick silently cursed him for sharing that bit of information, Melody's stick completely missed the cue ball, and she jerked upright.

Nick held out the other bottle. "I got you another beer."

After shooting the bartender a look that should have frozen him in his place, she grabbed the bottle from Nick's hand. "Your shot." Turning on her heel, she stomped to the other end of the pool table.

Smiling to himself as she upended the bottle and took a long drink, Nick eyed the colorful balls. There was nothing like alcohol to loosen a person's tongue.

Lining his stick up on the cue ball, Nick smacked it toward the four. He missed it entirely but did manage to hit the seven ball, which bounced off the other side of the table and rolled into the side pocket.

His opponent snorted. "If you meant that to happen, I'm a Houston debutante."

Catching her gaze with his, Nick smiled at her. "It's all part of my plan to lull you into complacency."

She flared her nostrils and stiffened.

Nick blinked.

In the dim light, her eyes looked like they had gold sparkles in them.

Then she broke eye contact and chugged more beer.

Nick missed his next shot.

As Melody set her beer down and began to line up her shot, Nick turned sideways to check out the rest of the bar. A couple of women had joined Melody's partner and the sheriff—their wives probably.

All four of them were staring at him.

Turning his back on them, Nick did some rapid recalculating. Obviously, people in this town, at least some of them, were far more protective of Melody Gray than he'd anticipated. He glanced toward the bar. The burly bartender had the same measuring look in his eyes as he leaned against his bar and stared. Earlier, when he'd pulled out that pump-action shotgun, Nick's blood had run cold. He'd had absolutely no doubt that it was loaded and the bartender would have used it.

As Nick concentrated Melody the hairs on the back of his neck rose. The tension in the bar that he'd originally attributed to Melody's altercation with Kenny hadn't dissipated. Instead, it was becoming thicker. Why?

Nonchalantly, Nick sipped more beer and forced his tense body to relax—at least to appear relaxed. The sheriff knew why he was in town. Nick had made a point of stopping by his office and explaining his presence right after he'd made his initial visit to Melody Gray's office. Local law enforcement wasn't always too happy about the presence of any federal officials, and Nick always let them know he was in town and why he was there. He got a lot more cooperation that way. This particular sheriff had been more than affable. He'd even pointed out the way to Melody's office. Of course, Nick had thanked him, and hadn't told the sheriff he'd already made

Melody's acquaintance. But, at that time, he hadn't thought he'd be in this town any longer than he'd been in the others he'd followed Jake Hurley through.

"You still playing or what?"

Nick wrenched his attention back to Melody. She was leaning back against a table, holding the longneck bottle in one hand and twirling her pool stick in the other.

She must have missed another shot.

He glanced over the table. All the striped balls were gone—and so were most of the solids. The black eight ball was still on the table, as were the red three and yellow one. "Been playing with my balls too, huh?" he commented in a voice only she could hear.

For a moment she gaped at him. Then a warm flush rose from her neck to her cheeks.

Smiling, he turned his back on her and studied the table—at least he pretended to study the table. From beneath hooded eyes, he glanced at the rest of the bar and its patrons. The two couples who'd stared at him so intently earlier were busy giving their orders to a waitress and the bar's owner was serving two new patrons sitting at the other end of the bar.

Still, the tension remained.

"Don't mind Bart," Melody said in a soft voice. "His bark is worse than his bite."

"Don't try to tell me that shotgun isn't loaded, or that he wouldn't have used it," Nick answered just as quietly as he pretended to contemplate his next shot.

Her chuckle danced up his spine. "It's loaded with rock salt but has barely enough powder to get the shot off. It would only sting a little."

Nick snorted, for the first time in a very long time not willing to trust his voice. What was so fascinating about this woman whom he hadn't even found attractive the first time he saw her? What was making her so desirable now?

"You know, if you line your shot to the three ball up on this side of the table and bank it off the end, it will roll down into this corner."

Nick glanced at her. "Easy for you to say."

"Come here. I'll show you." Grabbing his wrist, she dragged him to the other side of the table. "See, line up it up like this."

Before Nick had a chance to say anything else, she had him bending over the table while she lay on his back with her arms wrapped around him, her hands clasping his on the pool stick.

Her breasts were pressed flat against his back while her hips and thighs cradled his ass. Her sweetly subtle perfume surrounded him, tickling his senses with a promise of—what?

His cock twitched, and he had trouble concentrating on the balls on the table as the two between his legs began to tingle.

Her warm breath caressed his ear. "Just pull back and thrust your stick forward," she whispered huskily.

Thrust! That particular word brought pictures to his mind he didn't want to acknowledge. Sweat beading on his brow, Nick complied. The three ball reacted just as she said it would.

The sound of grumbling from behind the bar reached him. Sounded like the bartender was not at all happy with Melody's instruction.

"You feel pretty nice lying on my back like this," Nick murmured, "but the chance of rock salt from the bartender's shotgun peppering my ass isn't all that appealing."

"Oh!" Jerking herself up, she stepped back. "I'm sorry!" Grabbing her beer, she drained the last of the liquid from the bottle. Then she stared at him for a moment, her eyes widening. "Excuse me, I'll be right back." Spinning on her heel, she disappeared toward the ladies' room.

Expelling a deep breath, Nick drained his bottle and picked up her empty. One more, just one more beer, and he was sure he'd be able to find out what she wasn't telling him about Hurley.

When Melody reached the ladies' room, she pushed against the door. It didn't budge.

"Just a minute," a feminine voice called.

"Shit!" Without thinking twice, Melody entered men's room and locked the door behind her. Since it was still relatively early in the evening and Bart hadn't had a lot of customers yet, the men's room was empty—and clean. Bracing her hands against the sink, she stared at herself in the mirror.

Mate! Mate! Mate! cried her soul.

"Oh shut up!"

She raked her hair back with her right hand and continued to stare at herself. What was she going to do? Give in? Mate Nick Price? Her reflection grinned ruefully. "What if he doesn't want me?" she muttered aloud. Gods, he's human!

Sighing, she dropped her gaze to the floor. Damn but she needed to talk to somebody who didn't live in this town, somebody she trusted implicitly. Lifting her head, she looked back in the mirror. There was only one person she trusted more than she trusted herself. Pulling her cell phone out of her pocket, she punched in a number.

On the other end, the phone rang once, twice, five times, eight…

Melody blinked. "Come on. Pick up. I need you."

"Hello? Melody, is that you?"

Melody felt as if a huge weight had been lifted from her shoulders. Blinking away tears of relief, she swallowed once. "Belle, I was afraid you weren't there."

"Mel, what's wrong? Why is the reception so bad? These phones are supposed to be state-of-the-art."

"I'm in the men's room of the local bar."

"Men's room? Why in the world are you in the men's room?"

"Oh, Belle, I don't know what to do."

Her sister's voice became worried. "Mel, what's happened? Should I call Dad?"

"No! Not Dad! He can't help."

"Then what's wrong?"

"Belle, I've found my mate."

The voice that answered her was jubilant. "Mel! That's wonderful. Who is it?"

Melody didn't try to hide the sadness and uncertainty in her voice. "No, it isn't wonderful. He's a human. What's more, he's the CIA agent who's after Garth. Oh, Belle, what do I do?"

Chapter Nine

&

On the other end of the phone, Belle stared at the wall. "The fates sure are playing games with our family," she mumbled, mostly to herself. First they'd lost their mother, causing their father to suffer in loneliness for years until he'd found Moira. Before she'd accept him, their brother Kearnan had to chain his mate Serena to the bed, while her own Alex had had to overcome his and his pack's prejudice about the fact that her mother had been a full wolf and not a *Were*. Garth and his mate Eileen had been separated for years because her parents suffered from the same prejudice, and Eileen had been forced to mate a male who beat her before she and Garth were reunited. Now Melody's inner wolf had chosen a human who wanted to lock Garth in a cell and throw away the key. Damn, but their family had had more than its share of trials and tribulations before they'd each found their mates. *Brendan better dig a hole and hide in it for the rest of his life,* she added to herself. *At this rate, the roller coaster ride the fates will take him on will turn his gray hair white.*

Over on the sunny windowsill, Callie lifted her head. *Live your life as it unfolds.*

Belle glanced at the calico cat. "That's easy for you to say," she mumbled. "You're a cat."

Callie swiped a white paw with her pink tongue. *Life is not easy. Life is not hard. Life just is.*

"I don't have time to argue philosophy with you right now."

Standing, the cat stretched then jumped to the floor. *I do not know what philosophy is, but I do know life. Eat, sleep, mate. That is all. That is enough.*

Melody's sad voice slid into Belle's ear. "What did you say? Belle, are you still there? Who are you talking to? What am I going to do?"

Sighing, Belle turned her attention back to her sister. "Callie says to eat, sleep and mate. Maybe you should take her advice."

"Advice from a cat? My life is falling apart around me, and you're talking to your cat?"

As Belle watched her cat saunter across the floor and into the kitchen, she concentrated on her sister. Melody was one of the strongest women Belle knew. She'd never been this unsure about anything. Even when their mother had died, Melody had gathered her will, marshaled her sister and brothers, and kept their father from following their mother onto the moon paths. After they'd entered the human world, Melody had always been there for Belle, no matter what the problem. This had to be the first time in their lives that Melody didn't know what to do.

Belle chewed on her lip. Melody was a strong woman, and she'd always trusted her instincts before. It wasn't that she didn't know what to do. She didn't *want* to do it. "Mel, you have to trust yourself. We're more wolf than human. Trust the wolf in your soul. It knows what it's doing. It wouldn't have chosen this man if he weren't worthy."

"That's easy for you to say. You fell in love with a *Were*. This guy is *human*! Just how do you think he'll react when I go all furry on him, especially when he's hunting Garth so he can lock him up for the government to dissect?"

Belle concentrated on only one word her sister said. "Love? Do you love him?" Then she grimaced at the "Oh fuck" that leaped from the phone into her ear.

On the other end of the line, Melody pulled the phone away from her ear and gaped at it. Then she yelled, "Love him? Are you nuts? I don't even know him! I've only spoken to him like three times!"

And finger-fucked yourself as he watched, and practically melted over his back not fifteen minutes ago. Your nipples are still tingling, her conscience added in a sly tone.

Mate now! added her werewolf soul.

"That's not love, that's lust," she mumbled as she put the phone back to her ear.

"What was that about lust?" her sister asked.

"Nothing. You misunderstood."

"I doubt it. Lust was the first thing on my mind when I saw Alex."

"But Nick is *human*!" Melody repeated.

"So is Moira," Belle answered, "and look how happy she and Dad are. Besides, the blood transfusion will enhance his natural abilities and instincts enough to take anything you can dish out."

"He's black."

"Who gives a rat's ass about that? You're just trying to come up with excuses. Alex and Serena are Native American," Belle countered.

"What about him hunting Garth?"

Belle's laughter rolled through the phone. "Once your mate has the transfusion of your blood, he'll be almost as much of a *Were* as Garth. I don't think he'll want to be a scientific study either."

Her mate. Swallowing, Melody blinked back a tear. Even to herself, her voice sounded small. "What if he doesn't want me?"

At first, more silence. Then Belle's voice roared through the phone. "Doesn't want you? Are you kidding? Damn it, Melody, what's wrong with you? You're the most self-confident member of the family. Listen to yourself. You're whining like a cub stuck out in the rain!"

"I am not!"

"Then what would you call it?"

Melody stared at herself in the mirror. What *was* wrong with her? Why was she doubting herself, her *Were* self? Damn, she was acting like one of those wishy-washy, too-stupid-to-live heroines in a romance novel. The portion of her soul that was pure wolf had never been wrong. Somehow, someway, Nick Price was supposed to be her mate whether she liked it or not. Whether he liked it or not.

She stared at her pale face in the mirror. So be it.

A loud thumping on the door interrupted her contemplation. "Hey, you gonna be in there all night?"

Pulling her scattered thoughts together, Melody concentrated on the phone once more. "Belle, I have to go. Thanks for listening. You were a big help."

Before her sister could answer, Melody slapped the phone closed.

Her gaze connected with the condom machine on the wall.

She pursed her lips.

Mate, mate, mate, snarled her soul.

"Looks like I'm going to have to start drinking aconite tea again, or I'll be pregnant the next time I come into heat," she muttered as she dug into her pocket for change.

The man in the hallway stumbled back in surprise when Melody stepped out of the men's room.

Shoulders back, she smiled. "Sorry, but I really had to go." Pushing past him, she headed back to the bar.

Nick was leaning against the smooth oak bar. As she approached him, he held out another bottle of beer.

Taking it from him, she set it on the bar. Then she took his bottle from his hand and set that one on the bar too. "Put them on my tab, Bart." Grabbing Nick's wrist, she tried to pull him toward the back door. "Come on."

He didn't budge. "When I buy a lady a drink, I'm used to

her drinking it."

Huffing in exasperation, Melody said, "I've had enough, and I have something else to tell you."

That got his interest just as she knew it would.

"What?"

"Outside, if you don't mind." She added, "Please?"

For a moment he stared at her. Then he nodded. "Okay. I take it this is about the case I'm working on."

Melody nodded.

This time when she gave his wrist a tug, he followed her.

"Why the back door?"

"Sometimes Steve thinks he's my father."

"Steve?"

She pointed her chin in the direction of the booth where the two middle-aged couples were enjoying their dinners. "The sheriff."

Pulling Nick back through the hallway that led to the restrooms, Melody passed those and pushed the door at the end open, stepping out into the alley. As soon as Nick was outside, she closed the door.

The light above the door was dim, but then werewolves were better at seeing in the dark than humans were anyway. She had no trouble seeing the anticipation on Nick's face. She had a feeling he was anticipating something entirely different than what he was about to get.

"So what do you want…"

Melody didn't give him a chance to finish. Shoving him against the back wall of the bar, she plastered her body against his, wrapped her arms around his neck, and kissed him—long, slowly, and thoroughly. She slid her tongue around his lips and when he opened his mouth, she chuckled low in her throat.

Though he stiffened, he didn't fight her.

Mine! the wolf in her soul howled joyfully.

As she slid her tongue into his mouth, she felt his cock harden against her thigh.

However, he didn't fall helplessly into her arms.

Wrapping his fingers around her upper arms, he untangled his tongue from hers and pushed her away. "What the fuck are you doing?"

Melody stared into his face. He was only about an inch taller than she so staring him in the eye was no problem. Damn but he had to have phenomenal control to break that kiss. Her insides were shaking and rolling around like gelatin. "Kissing you," she finally said, slightly perturbed by the breathlessness in her voice. "You do know what kissing is, don't you? Or have you spent your entire adult life chasing after people?"

He completely ignored her comment. "Why?" was all he said.

Sticking out her bottom lip, Melody forced out a small puff of air to blow some strands of hair off her face. Shit but he was stubborn. "Because you're just about the sexiest man I've ever met. Why fight the attraction?"

As she smiled then licked her upper lip with the tip of her tongue, Nick felt his already hard cock stiffen even more. To have that tongue on him…

His balls tightened.

He fought the urge to wrap his arms around her.

"Why?" he asked again.

"I just told you why."

"No, why the attraction? It certainly wasn't there the first day I walked into your office."

Her slow shrug raised her breasts then let them fall. In the dim light, he could see her nipples poking against the shirt she wore. "I guess you grew on me." Since the lower half of her body was still flush against his, she brushed her thigh against his hard cock. "I guess I've grown on you, too."

Nick shook his head. "Listen..."

She leaned her face close to his. "Will you stop trying to analyze this...attraction...and just enjoy yourself?" She slid her tongue along his lips and swiveled her hips against his thigh and now-aching cock.

Nick stiffened, sucked in his breath, then spat, "Fuck it!" Throwing away caution and his once unbreakable rule never to get involved with anyone he was investigating, Nick gave in to the urges he felt every time he saw Melody Gray. Spinning them both around, he pushed her against the door and attacked her mouth with his.

She counterattacked by stabbing her tongue into his mouth, then sucking his into hers.

Their teeth clicked and clashed. Their tongued sparred and parried.

He cupped her breast and squeezed.

She shuddered and wrapped one leg around his thigh.

Groaning, Nick opened his mouth wider, his tongue now dancing with hers. His cock was harder than it had ever been and his balls were on fire. Never had he wanted—no, needed to bury himself in a woman so badly.

Somehow she slipped her hand between them, something he didn't think was possible considering how closely their bodies were plastered together, jerked his jeans open, slid her hand down the front of his pants, grabbed his cock and pulled it free of his boxers, her warm hand circling and caressing the head.

"You're gonna make me come too soon," Nick moaned into her mouth.

"Off. Get these damned jeans off," she demanded against his mouth as she lowered her leg and jerked at the waistband of his jeans. The upper portion of his cock inched free. "You are so damn hard!" she mumbled against his mouth. "I need your cock."

With far more strength than he thought a woman could have, she spun him around so that his back was against the wall, fell to her knees, pulled his pants and underwear down to his ankles, and sucked his cock into her mouth.

"Oh Christ," he groaned. He spread his legs and tilted his head back against the wall, and slammed his fists back against it. Her tongue was magic, her mouth molten heat as she sucked and nibbled. He thrust his hips forward and she sucked him in.

He slid his cock deeper into her mouth as she sucked. Gently, she raked her teeth along him as he slid back out. The sharp pressure had his stomach muscles rippling. She sucked his cock back in and replaced her teeth with her tongue.

Nick groaned and buried his hands in her hair.

As she slid her tongue around him, she cupped his balls and rolled them in her hand.

It was too much. He had to bury himself inside her.

Grabbing her shoulders, Nick pushed her mouth off his cock, slipped his hands under her arms, lifted her back to her feet, and spun them both around again so her back was flat against the wall. "Clothes. Off. Now."

He didn't wait for her to strip. Shoving her shirt up over her breasts, he popped the clasp on the front of her bra, bent, nipped a taut nipple, then sucked it into his mouth.

When he nipped her already tender nipple, Melody pounded her fist against the wall. Oh gods, when had she ever wanted a man so much!

She tore at the buttons on her jeans, popping a few in the process. Shoving the jeans down over her hips, she grabbed his cock again.

When he slid his hand between her thighs, she arched into it and his fingers slipped inside of her. She ground down against them.

"Christ, you're wet."

Nuzzling his neck, Melody nipped his earlobe. "I want you, inside me, now!"

"Not as much as I want to be inside you!" He rubbed his cock against the inside of her thigh.

"Condom," she gasped, "in my pocket!"

It only took him moments to bend down, fish the small plastic package from her pocket, tear it open and unroll the condom down onto himself.

"Now, baby. Now I'm ready for you," he breathed into her ear as he buried his face in her neck.

Melody spread her legs wider then cursed with frustration when the jeans tangled around her ankles wouldn't let her lift her leg to wrap around his hips.

There were drawbacks to wearing boots.

Her tangled jeans weren't a hindrance. Cupping her ass, Nick lifted her against the wall and, using his knee to spread her thighs as wide as he could, he dropped her onto his steel-hard cock.

Wrapping her arms around his neck, Melody sobbed into his mouth as her internal muscles stretched to accommodate his thick cock. She shuddered as he lifted her and impaled her again. Squeezing her cunt muscles tight, she twisted her hips as she nipped his shoulder. "Yes, oh yes. Harder. Harder."

He heaved upward and thrust into her.

Her ass rubbed against the rough wood of the wall.

She didn't care.

His body pressed against hers, Nick continued to grind his hips and thrust his cock into her as deeply as he could. "Fuck, baby, your pussy's hot and wet. That's it, squeeze me. Twist your hips. That's it. Faster."

The scent of sex surrounded them and the werewolf in Melody's soul howled with joy. She nipped his other shoulder and held on to him more tightly. "Deeper. Harder," she moaned.

His fingers slid down the crack in her ass.

As pressure built deep inside of her, her nipples tightened in the cool air. The muscles of her abdomen shuddered.

Melody sobbed. "Now. Oh, now!"

Bursts of light flashed behind her eyes.

Nick swiveled his hips and rammed himself into her over and over. He wasn't being gentle, but from the way she kept nipping his neck and shoulders, he quickly determined she liked rough sex. He certainly didn't care. His burning balls were tight against his body and his cock was ready to explode. She was squirming and bouncing against him, her hot, wet pussy grasping his cock far more tightly than any other woman's ever had.

As much as he wanted to prolong his and her pleasure, his body refused to cooperate. He couldn't hold back. When she screamed, "Now!" he surged upward one last time. His loud groan echoed her scream as a volcano of heat erupted up through his cock. Roaring filled his ears and his knees shook. Burying his face in her neck, he was forced to lean against her so he didn't collapse.

Christ, but no woman had ever affected him like this.

Chapter Ten

ꟿ

Melody sucked in deep breaths. Once her heart stopped trying to leap out of her chest, she gasped, "Let me down."

After a deep breath, Nick eased away from her and loosened his hold on her ass—after he was sure her wobbling legs would support her.

She flattened her hands against his chest and swirled her fingertips against his firm pecs. "I think we should go back to my place."

"My hotel room is closer," Nick murmured, his eyelids half closed as he smiled at her. He cupped her buttock and squeezed.

"Hmm. Oh yes." She nipped his neck.

His hand tightened on her ass. "I never pictured you as a biter."

She dragged her tongue over the spot she'd just nipped. Hmm, but he tasted good. "You don't like it?"

His growled "I like it" sent shivers twisting and twirling up and down her spine.

Melody slid her hand down his arm. "Let's go."

Stepping away from her, he shoved his cock into his jeans.

As she pulled up her own jeans, Melody chuckled. "Tight fit?"

He grinned back. "Tight enough. You ready?" He held out his hand.

Maneuvering her bra down over her tender breasts, Melody fastened the clasp, pulled her shirt into place, and slipped her hand in his. "More than you know." The wolf in her soul was practically humming with satisfaction while the grin he gave her in the dim light had her stomach muscles tightening all over again. She shivered.

"Cold?"

She shook her head. "Anticipating."

His deep chuckle set her werewolf soul howling to have sex right there in the alley again.

Melody squashed the urge. Once a night up against a rough, wooden wall was enough, especially when a comfortable bed was close by.

At the mouth of the alley, a dark shadow loomed against the glow from the electric lanterns hanging from the bar's porch roof. "You fuckin' bitch! I can smell him all over you! You're mine!"

Melody's snarl reverberated off the walls of the alley. Their assailant's scent was unmistakable. "When will you get it through your thick skull that I don't belong to anybody, Kenny!"

The dull gleam of a knife glinted in a stray beam of light. "If I can't have you, no one will!"

As Melody moved forward, Nick simultaneously tried to push her behind him and step forward to defend her. Her movement knocked him off balance, and they fell forward together.

Holding the knife low, Kenny leaped toward them. His unearthly howl shattered the relative peace of the street as he slashed through muscle and sinew.

Nick grunted as blood spurted from the deep cut on the inside of his upper thigh. "You fucking bastard," he swore as he untangled himself from Melody and lunged forward. His fist connected with Kenny's chin and the other man flew backward.

"Damn it, Nick, stop moving. You're bleeding," Melody growled as she stepped past him.

"Get back before he stabs you, too!" Nick commanded as he clamped one hand over his wound and struggled to his feet. He knew he was bleeding—too much if he was any judge of the warm sticky liquid spurting from between his fingers. The fucking asshole must have nicked an artery. He tried to grab Melody with his free hand, but she eluded him.

As warm liquid rolled down his leg, he stumbled. Gathering his strength, he stepped after Melody. Again he stumbled, then fell to his knees. "Fuck, this is worse than I thought," he mumbled. With his free hand—it seemed to take forever to reach his ankle—he grabbed at the revolver hidden in the holster under his jeans. As his vision blurred, he was able to grab onto it with his third try and yank it free. Raising it, he blinked to clear his vision, then shook his head and blinked again. His hand wavered and he cursed. No way was he steady enough to shoot at Kenny with Melody so close. He couldn't guarantee his aim. There was only one other thing to do. Pointing the gun at the wall opposite him, he fired. The explosion echoed through the alley.

As the gun fell from his weakening grasp, he collapsed against a trash can. The shot was loud enough to wake the dead, and they were in the alley next to the restaurant where the sheriff was eating. He would not ignore what he'd heard. If Melody could stay away from that knife and hold her own for a few minutes…

Once again Nick blinked to clear his vision and cursed silently. He was losing blood too fast. Melody and her attacker were nothing more than a misty white and brown haze in front of him.

He squinted and tried to concentrate on the fight he couldn't see.

Somewhere close by, a dog yelped.

As he leaned his head back against the trash can, Nick grunted. A barking dog. Good. In a town this small, peopled looked to see what a dog was barking at.

Then, as another revolver shot blasted through the silence of the night, blackness closed around him.

When the sound of the first gunshot exploded around them, Melody kicked the knife out of Kenny's hand as he froze momentarily. It flew through the air and skidded away through the darkness. "Okay, asshole, now fight fair."

Without bothering to remove any clothing, Melody shifted. Silvery-white haze swirled and sparkled around her as her clothing fell to the ground. Seconds later, a white wolf snarled and leaped toward Kenny.

Stumbling back from Melody's attack, her opponent also shifted. However, he attained his wolf form tangled in his human clothing. As Melody's teeth scored a deep slash in his side, he yelped with pain.

Her teeth bared, Melody leaped away from Kenny and spun around to resume her attack. He had attacked her mate! He would die!

However, before she could close in on him, another shot shattered the night as, two feet in front of her, a bullet kicked up dust then ricocheted into the restaurant's outer wall.

"Shift back, Melody," the sheriff commanded in a low voice. "Now! Before any humans see you! That's an order! You too, Kenny."

Snarling with displeasure, Melody nevertheless complied. The sheriff was Alpha of the Pack here, and she would obey him.

"What the hell is going on?" the sheriff growled once they were human again.

Both started talking at the same time.

"She fucked another…"

"He knifed…."

"Knife? Who got knifed?"

As she was pulling on her clothing, Melody froze. Nick

was being strangely quiet.

"Nick!" Half dressed, she leaped back into the darkness.

When Melody reached his side, her heart seemed to leap into her throat.

He was sitting in a puddle of his own blood, a puddle that was slowly expanding.

As she searched for his wound, the other two men's voices followed her into the darkness.

"She fucked a human, Sheriff. She's my mate and she fucked a human!" Kenny snarled. "He deserved to die."

Her keen hearing picked up the sound of quick steps and that of a body being slammed against a solid wall. "Die?" the sheriff snarled. "You killed him? You killed a CIA agent? You mother-fucking asshole! You've put the entire Pack in danger. I should put a bullet in your head right now."

The sound of Bart's shotgun being pumped echoed through the alley from the darkness. He must have come out the back door. His voice was low and deadly. "Just move out of the way, Sheriff, and I'll take care of that for you."

As she slid her hand up Nick's thigh, she pushed his hand aside. Blood spurted against her palm. "Sheriff! Send someone for the doctor! Nick is spurting blood from his femoral artery."

"He's already on the way. I sent Dan for him before I came out. Keep your hand on the wound, Melody. It's the best we can do until Doc gets here. And you, Kenny, if he dies, you do too. You've compromised the safety of the Pack. This town could end up crawling with federal agents. Every *Were* will have to leave."

"I don't care. She's my mate! Mine! Nobody else can have her! No *Were,* no human! I'll kill them all first." Kenny's labored breathing rattled through the silence.

"He's crazy, Sheriff. Best put him out of his misery," Bart said.

The sheriff's sigh rolled around Melody while she pressed

both hands against Nick's wound. "Much as I'd like to, Bart, I can't. He has the right to defend himself to the entire Pack, and they have the right to decide. I'll keep him locked up until we can gather for a meeting."

A new voice joined the sheriff's. "You need me?"

Melody didn't give the sheriff a chance to answer. "Back here, Cail. Nick is bleeding to death."

"Kenny stabbed the CIA agent," the sheriff added. "Melody says it looks pretty bad. After I get Kenny locked up, I'll be over to the clinic to see how he's doing, Doc."

A flash of lightning split the sky and thunder rumbled.

"Would you two stop talking, damn it! Cail, get back here!"

In seconds, the doctor was kneeling at her side.

Bart had taken his shotgun back into the building and returned with a large flashlight, the beam of which he now directed on Nick's wound.

"Christ, this is bad," the doctor muttered. "Melody, keep that pressure on the wound while I get a tourniquet around his thigh. I can't do anything else here." Once his quick first aid was applied, he glanced at Melody. "You better finish dressing before Ben and Dan get here with the stretcher. I need them concentrating on carrying this guy to the clinic not on your breasts."

Another flash of lightning lit the alley. More thunder rolled around the sky.

Melody wrenched her eyes from Nick's pale face. "What?" She looked down at herself. Her naked, blood-spattered breasts shone pale in the light of the flashlight. "Oh, yeah. Right." Lunging to her feet, she found her shirt and yanked it over her head and down over her breasts. She was stuffing her bra in a pants pocket as the two humans arrived with a stretcher. As they set it down next to Nick, Dan gasped and blanched at the sight of all the blood. Another bright flash of lightning lit up the sky. More thunder boomed. A fat raindrop landed on Melody's arm.

"Just what I need," the doctor growled. "Forecast is calling for storms all night. There's no way a helicopter can get up here for this guy, and I doubt if he'll be stable enough to put in any kind of vehicle." He glanced at the men holding the stretcher. "Damn it, Dan. You better not faint on me. You've helped butcher enough deer that the sight of blood shouldn't bother you."

Dan's swallow was audible to everyone. "But that ain't human blood, Doc."

"Christ. Bart, give Dan the flashlight and help Ben lift this guy onto the stretcher."

More rain drops fell.

Melody hovered. "What should I do?"

"Just stay out of the way."

"Now wait a minute, Cail. Nick is…"

"Damn it, Melody. It can wait. If you want him alive, you'll stay out of my way! We have to get him to the clinic before it rains harder than it already is. This wound is bad enough. The last thing he needs is to be drenched and catch pneumonia."

Snarling, Melody stepped back. In his own way, the doctor was as much an Alpha as the sheriff. Gods, but sometimes she hated Alphas.

As Nick was carried away, the rain fell harder.

Half an hour later, the doctor stared down at his patient and shook his head. "That's the best I can do. I've repaired the artery as best I can. It should be fine until I can get him to a hospital, but he needs more blood." He nodded his head at the almost- empty bag hanging next to Nick's bed. "That's the last bag I've got."

Melody paced back and forth. Nick could die!

Mine, howled her soul. *He is mine! Help him!*

Melody didn't hesitate. If Nick died, how would she live without him? "Give him mine."

The sound of a board creaking in the next room was more than audible as both the sheriff and doctor stared at Melody.

Fisting her hands on her hips, she stared back. "You heard me."

"Melody…"

She flared her nostrils and leaned forward. "Don't 'Melody' me, Cail. He's my mate. He'd get my blood anyway."

"Now, Melody…"

"I'm not going to listen to you either, Sheriff."

The doctor stepped away from the bed and stopped before Melody.

She met his gaze without flinching.

"Mel, he has to accept you and your blood of his own free will. You can't force him."

She shook her head. Her werewolf soul was howling with pain and fury. *Save him! Save him! Save him!* "I'm not forcing him. I'm saving his life."

The doctor raked his fingers through his hair.

"No," Melody said before he—or the sheriff—could say anything. "I know you only want what's best for me, but that's Nick. All the gods know that I fought against this mating. For Pete's sake, he's human, and he wants to turn my brother over to the government. Do you really think I wanted this to happen?"

Neither man answered her.

"It's done. He's my mate. You both know what that's like. If your mates were in the same predicament, it would tear your souls out not to help them and you know it."

Both men sighed.

A long shudder raced up and down Melody's body. Tears welled up and she tried to blink them away. A few escaped and rolled down her cheeks. "Cail, please, he's my mate."

The doctor sighed again and shook his head.

The sheriff lifted his hat from a nearby chair. "She's right, Doc. She won't be able to live with herself if she doesn't help him." He settled his hat on his head, pursed his lips, then smiled. "Besides, once he has some of her blood, he'll practically be *Were* himself. He won't be turning her brother over to the government, not if he doesn't want to become an experiment himself."

After a few seconds of staring at Nick's too-pale face, the doctor nodded. "Okay. Lie down on the bed next to his, Melody. One pint from you will be like two from a human, and his wound will heal well enough that he won't need to go to a hospital once the *Were* blood is in his system. Add to that the fact that your mother was pure wolf, well, we're going to have to watch him carefully."

Stress flowed out of Melody as both her muscles and her mind relaxed. With her blood, Nick would live.

Chapter Eleven

ജ

The sound of someone breathing dragged Nick from unconsciousness. Before he even opened his eyes, he knew Melody was close to his left side. Her scent gave her away—or at least the fragrance of her perfume did.

"Did you take a bath in the stuff?" he mumbled as he dragged his eyes open.

Joy blossomed in her voice. "Nick?"

He blinked a few times then focused on her face as she leaned over him. Her features seemed sharper somehow, clearer, gold-flecked blue eyes, soft ivory skin, kissable lips. Her scent was almost overpowering, yet, for some reason, more enticing than anything he'd ever experienced. He chose to ignore it as the memory of the fight in the alley surfaced. Blood, lots of it.

He'd been stabbed—badly.

"What happened to the guy who attacked us?"

"He's in jail."

Grunting affirmatively, Nick tried to touch his wound and discovered his wrists were strapped into thick, leather, wool-lined cuffs attached to the side railings of the bed.

"What the hell?"

"You wouldn't leave your wound alone. You kept trying to pull at your stitches or jerk the IV out, so the doctor had to strap your wrists down."

Her answer made sense, but Nick glared at her anyway. He didn't like being confined. "You can release me now. How long have I been out?"

Her smile seemed to light the entire room. "You've been

unconscious for about thirty-six hours."

Nick looked down and moved his leg tentatively.

A dull ache rewarded his efforts. It didn't hurt as much as he'd expected.

He looked up at Melody again. Still smiling, she was staring down at his chest. Then she licked her lips.

Her nipples were poking against her red tee shirt.

Her smiled widened even more as her gaze wandered down his body and back up again to focus on his chest. "You are definitely ripped."

At that moment, Nick realized he was naked except for the sheet that covered him.

He heard her small intake of breath when his cock twitched.

"You know," she said as she leaned over and traced a single finger up his bare chest to his shoulder then down his arm to his wrist restraints, "my brother handcuffed his mate to a bed. I'll bet the sex was fantastic."

His cock did more than twitch. A tent rose at the juncture of his thighs.

He did his best to ignore it. "Good for them. Now let me loose."

Her gaze meandered up his chest to his face. She licked her lips again. "I don't think so."

Nick flared his nostrils. The spicy, enticing scent of her arousal rolled off her and engulfed him.

The tent between his thighs moved.

"I don't think *he* wants me to let you go," she said in a low voice while she reached down and dragged a single finger up his sheet-covered cock.

The feel of the soft cotton rubbing against his skin tantalized him as much as her scent. Still, he fought to retain control of both his body and the situation. He used the low, dangerous tone of voice he usually reserved for desperate situations. "Melody. Let me go. Now."

She ignored him and her chuckle added fuel to the fire burning in his groin. It spread upward to his stomach when she stopped tracing his cock through the sheet and walked her fingers up his clenching abdomen to his waist where the top of the sheet lay. She hooked it with a finger and dragged it slowly down his abdomen, his groin, his hips, his thighs.

Cool air tickled his thighs as his cock danced this way and that, aching for her touch.

She ignored it.

Eyes narrowed, he watched her face.

She licked her lips as her gaze drifted from one part of his body to another. "I've never seen such a delicious color on a human before—like rich, dark caramel. Do you taste as good?"

Nick glared at her. Why wasn't he in control of this situation? Being tied down shouldn't make any difference. It had happened before. "The other night should have answered that question."

Her smile was lazy and indolent. "I was too busy *feeling* to think about *tasting*." She trailed two fingers up his stomach and chest then twirled them around the smattering of tight, black curls there. "Your hair is so soft." She looked up into his face. "It wouldn't hurt you to grow some on your head, you know."

Like a butterfly flitting from flower to flower, her delicate fingers landed here and there on his chest.

"I like my head the way it is."

Her fingers slid down over his abdomen again.

His stomach muscles shuddered while his cock jerked again.

Chuckling, she grasped the sheet and pulled it down to his ankles. "I like the hair on your legs too, especially here, on the inside of the thigh."

As she dragged her fingers along the inside of his unhurt

thigh, she brushed against his balls.

They tingled and tightened.

"Damn it, Melody!"

She smiled up at him again. "Yes?"

Hands fisted so that his knuckles were white, Nick strained against the thick leather cuffs that held him to the bed.

They didn't give an inch.

He bared his teeth. "Let. Me. Go."

Bending over, she braced her hands on his chest, stared into his face, and said, "No." Then, after straightening, she pulled her shirt over her head.

Both ivory breasts bounced and her pebbled, pink nipples stared at him.

She unfastened her jeans, slid them and her panties down her legs and kicked them off. "I've always wondered what it would be like to make love to someone who was tied down," she said with a small pant. "Haven't you?"

Nick's gaze was glued to her crotch, to the silky, silver curls and velvety, red lips below them. The fragrance of her arousal was stronger now, more tantalizing—almost to the point where he could taste her. She smelled of untamed primeval heat and passion, of a time when sex was a challenge, a victory, and a defeat—all at the same time.

At that moment, Nick stopped trying to control the urges of his body. Only God knew why, but he wanted her more than he'd wanted any other woman. The memory of their lovemaking in the alley had only whetted his appetite for her, not satisfied it. He needed more, much more.

Her silvery hair fell forward and caressed his thighs when she bent over and sucked his cock into her mouth.

"Christ!" A bolt of electricity shot up his back and his stomach muscles clenched.

Her mouth was warm and wet, her tongue taunting and teasing as she danced it up, down and around his erection.

Then she lifted her head and smiled her sultry smile. "You do taste good—hot, spicy and all male. But I want to do more than taste you. I want to feel your hard cock deep inside me, filling and stretching me until I don't know where I end and you begin."

Before he could say anything, she crawled onto the bed and straddled him.

Nostrils flaring and stomach muscles tightening even more, Nick watched as she slowly lowered herself onto his hot, throbbing erection, watched as his dark cock disappeared into her ivory white body. His senses whirled, more alive than they had ever been before. Sight, smell, sound, touch, taste—all were more sensitive than ever.

And he gloried in them.

Forgetting everything except how wet and slick and hot she felt around his cock, Nick gave in to physical pleasure. "That's it, baby," he growled as she raised and lowered herself again and then again and again, faster each time. "Screw yourself down. Ride me—hard."

Head thrown back, she complied. Cupping her breasts, she squeezed her nipples.

"Play with your nipples, baby. Squeeze them harder."

Clenching and unclenching his fists, Nick struggled to free himself as Melody's internal muscles tightened around his cock, squeezed it, then released it as she pushed herself upward. But his bonds held and, as much as he wanted to touch her, he couldn't do more than caress the smooth skin of her spread thighs with the tips of his fingers. Still, watching her cupping her own breasts and playing with her nipples was almost as good as touching her himself.

"Come on, baby. Pinch your nipples. Yeah, like that."

She complied. Her nipples lengthened and hardened into rosy pebbles.

Nick's own nipples began to ache and his stomach muscles clenched as he watched her fuck herself on his cock.

"Come on, baby. Ride me harder, faster."

Lifting her arms over her head, Melody rose, arched her back, swiveled her hips, and screwed herself back down onto his cock.

Ignoring the quick stab of pain in his thigh, Nick groaned and lifted his hips. His balls were burning and his cock ached more than it ever had. "Harder, baby, harder. Ride me harder!"

She complied and dropped her arm. Her fingers found her clit and rubbed both it and his cock.

"Yes, baby, play with your clit."

The way her fingers stroked and danced over both of them had Nick gritting his teeth. Watching her play with herself had him straining against his bonds. He wanted his hands between her thighs, his fingers teasing her clit. He growled deep in his throat, a sound he'd never made before, but he didn't think about it, didn't care that his body didn't seem the same as it had been before. All he could concentrate on was the woman screwing herself onto his cock. Even the dull ache in his leg faded away until his world consisted only of the feeling spreading outward and upward from his groin. Sweat beaded on his forehead and his body became slick as he pumped his hips upward. Bursts of light flashed behind his eyes.

"Harder, baby," he repeated. "Ride me harder."

Both arms now crossed over her head, Melody did just that. Squeezing his hips with her thighs, she screwed herself down onto his cock then swiveled her hips again. His cock was rock-hard and it stretched and filled her more deeply every time she slid down onto it.

"Oh gods!"

"That's it, baby. You're slick and wet. Come for me, baby. Come for me." He pushed his hips up as hers came down.

Another groan escaped from Melody and she cupped her breasts again. She flared her nostrils and inhaled the scent of his arousal. Her breath caught in her throat when the muscles in his arms and shoulders bulged as he tried to wrench free of the leather cuffs that bound him to the bed. He bared his teeth and jerked harder, but those bonds were made to hold even the most powerful werewolf.

Nick Price was at her mercy, and that was the most potent aphrodisiac she'd ever experienced.

Panting, his arms still straining, he arched his hips even more. "Come on, baby. You got me hot, so hot. I'm ready to come." He pushed his cock as deeply into her body as he could.

Shuddering at how deeply he'd thrust his cock into her, Melody stared down into his face. Sweat beaded his brow. His dark, chocolaty gaze was locked on her groin. His nostrils flared. Quick breaths escaped his partially open mouth. He licked his lips.

Melody groaned. Oh, to have that tongue on her clit. She lifted herself completely off his cock and rolled off the side of the bed.

"What the fuck..." Anger and shock rumbled in his voice.

Turning around, Melody swung her leg over his torso. "I want your tongue," she moaned. Then she slid her mouth over his cock.

As she sucked on him, she inched her body back until he could reach her clit with his tongue. He lapped once, twice, and she shuddered. Then he lifted his head and sucked on her.

"More," she moaned around his cock. "More."

His warm breath teased her clit and cunt. He lapped her, sucked on her. "You taste like passion—hot, wild passion." He slid his tongue into her cunt and sucked harder.

Lost in passion, Melody sucked his cock as deeply as she could, trailed her tongue up and down, nibbled on the dark head and reveled in the salty taste of his precum.

The werewolf in her soul howled with triumph.

He dropped his head. "Ride me, baby. Ride me again."

Panting, she gave his cock one last, long lick, then spun around. Her pussy was wet and slick and slid easily down onto him.

He swiveled his hips.

As she reveled in the feelings rushing through her body, Melody noticed the quick flash of pain in his eyes.

His thigh! She'd been concentrating solely on her pleasure and forgotten completely about his injury.

Closing her eyes, she increased her pace and pumped herself up and down faster and faster. As much as she wanted to draw out their pleasure even more, she wasn't about to aggravate his injury when it was healing so well.

"Oh gods, yes!"

Sliding the fingers of her right hand down through the curls of her pubis, she rubbed her clit with her middle finger—once, twice, three times—and exploded with ecstasy when her internal muscles locked around the rock-hard cock buried deeply within her.

Beneath her, Nick cried out and shuddered as he reached his own orgasm.

Trembling, Melody melted onto Nick's prone body. Sighing, she nuzzled his neck. For a time, their hearts pounded in unison. As the minutes ticked by, their hearts slowed, their breathing eased.

Feeling more content than she ever had in her life, Melody pushed herself up, propped her arms on Nick's chest, and looked down into his face.

His expression was guarded and shuttered as he looked back up at her.

Smiling, she kissed his mouth.

Lifting her head, she looked down into his face again.

Before she could say anything, however, a loud pounding exploded into the room followed by an equally loud voice,

"Melody, open the damn door!"

Lifting herself off the bed, she stared at the door. Damn it, why did the doctor have to show up now?

Chapter Twelve

ꙮ

Nick lay impotently on the bed as more thuds reverberated around the room and Melody began to yank her clothing on. When she turned toward the door, he snapped, "Christ, Melody, cover me!"

Stopping in her tracks, she spun around and stared at him.

He lay naked on the bed, his now limp cock curled over his balls.

She smiled. "You look good enough to eat. I didn't get enough of a taste."

"Melody!"

She didn't hide the exasperation in her voice. "Jeez, Nick. He's a doctor and he's seen you naked already." Nevertheless, she stepped to the side of the bed and jerked the sheet up to his hips. "That better?" She also pressed the button that raised the top half of the bed.

Nick snorted. At least he wouldn't be lying flat on his back while he talked to the doctor.

More loud knocks rattled the door. "I'm coming, I'm coming," she said as she pulled her tee shirt over her head.

As Nick watched her ass cheeks dip back and forth as she sauntered to the door, he shook his head a bit to try to clear his thoughts. What the fuck was he doing with this woman? Christ but she was more becoming more and more appealing. Ridiculous! He wasn't interested in any one woman, especially one so—skinny. Was he?

When she reached the door, she unlocked it then jumped back out of the way as it was flung open.

"Christ, Melody," was all the doctor said to her. "Mr. Price, I'm sorry I wasn't here when you woke up, but I had another emergency. How are you feeling?" He stopped for a moment, his nostrils flaring. No one could miss the odor of sex floating around the room.

Frustrated at his lack of control over the entire situation, Nick didn't keep the anger from his voice. "Unfasten these restraints. Now!"

The eyebrows on the young doctor's face rose, and he glanced at Melody.

She smiled and shrugged.

Nick had no trouble hearing the quick curse the doctor mumbled as he bent over first one wrist then the other. "I'm sorry, Mr. Price. You kept trying to scratch your stitches or pull the IV out of the back of your hand."

Nick rubbed his wrists. "What IV?"

"I took it out before I left early this morning. You didn't need it anymore." Sitting down on the side of the bed, the doctor flipped the sheet off Nick's injured thigh, removed the bandage, and probed the wound. "Very good. Almost healed."

Nick leaned forward. "Almost healed?" That was impossible. "I thought it was bad."

Rising, the doctor nodded. "It was."

"If it was so serious, what am I still doing here? Why wasn't I evacuated to a hospital?"

"We had a major storm system come through right after you were stabbed. There was no way to get a helicopter here, and I didn't want you riding down bumpy mountain roads with a cut as bad as yours. The artery was nicked and you were losing a lot of blood."

"How much?"

"You needed three pints to get you back to where I felt you were out of danger."

Crossing his arms over his chest, Nick stared at the

doctor. "Didn't know you had a blood bank here."

"We don't. I didn't have time to check your blood type, so I took a pint each from the two men who carried you over—they were both O positive, and—Melody donated a pint."

Nick grunted and glanced over at the woman who confused him more than any other he'd ever met. Suddenly his eyes blurred and a black mist covered them. When he blinked, it was gone.

"Is something wrong?" The doctor's voice was concerned.

Nick put his palm to his forehead and blinked a few more times. "No. Nothing."

Pulling a pen light from the pocket of his white coat, the doctor shined it in both eyes and grunted. "Considering you've been flat on your back for a day and a half and lost as much blood as you have, a bit of dizziness wouldn't be surprising."

"I want my clothes."

"The ones you were wearing when you were brought here were covered with blood and had to be cut off. I asked the sheriff to go to your motel room to get you some. Mabel wouldn't let anyone else into a guest's room without permission."

Nick didn't bother to hide his displeasure, though he did have to agree with the doctor's reasoning. He hadn't left anything important lying around, but he did have a rented fax machine set up. Who knew what kind of information had arrived while he'd been unconscious? And the local sheriff was undoubtedly the kind of lawman who'd check out any faxes. This was his jurisdiction and he'd want to find out what Nick was up to. Nick had known at their first meeting that the sheriff was a smart man who knew there was more to the story Nick had given him. If there were faxes in Nick's motel room, the sheriff would read them. Nick would do the same thing in the sheriff's position.

As the scent of another person drifted into the clinic, the

black mist again blinded Nick. Sweat broke out on his forehead and his stomach churned.

He swallowed once, twice, and controlled the sudden nausea. The blackness behind his eyes disappeared.

Melody's voice broke through his concentration. "Nick? Are you okay?"

A new voice invaded his consciousness. "Somebody here need some clothes?"

Opening his eyes, Nick saw the stranger who'd strolled half-naked so confidently around Melody's house. Again his stomach churned—this time with anger. At the very least, this guy had seen Melody naked. If he ever touched her again…

"Who the hell are you?" Nick growled.

Smile disappearing, the gray-haired stranger pulled up short.

"Nick!" Melody exclaimed. "This is Brendan, my brother."

As soon as she identified the stranger, Nick saw the resemblance in their features and their silvery-blond hair, though Melody's was much lighter. His tense muscles relaxed and he cursed himself as they did so. Why should he care who this guy was? "The one who handcuffs women to beds?"

All three people in the room with him gaped for a few seconds, then Melody's brother burst into laughter. "No, that's Kearnan. Unlike him, I don't have to chain women to my bed. They're perfectly happy to be there in the first place." He tossed some clothing onto Nick's lap. "The sheriff asked me to bring these since I was coming here anyway. He had a traffic accident to deal with." He glanced at the doctor. "You might have some more customers for your clinic, Doc."

The doctor nodded but didn't leave. Instead all three continued to stare at Nick.

Nick stared back and considered what he'd learned in the last few minutes. Melody had two brothers. As soon as he'd become suspicious of Melody, he'd sent a fax back to headquarters requesting information about her. He'd received very little, only her present location and job—and the fact that her father owned one of the most profitable fragrance companies in the country. Now he knew she had two brothers. However, when he'd first arrived in town, he'd found out everything he could about Melody. He knew she had no relatives living in the area. So what was her brother Brendan doing here now, and why had he been here a few days ago? A simple visit? Or was there something else going on? And did they always walk around each other naked? What were they, nudists?

Nick shifted in the bed. Considering he was lying naked except for a sheet with three people staring at him, going on the offensive might be his best bet. He locked gazes with Melody's brother. "What the hell are you doing here?"

The other man glanced at his sister. "You haven't explained things to him yet, have you?"

Melody shook her head. "I haven't had a chance."

Nick's stomach rolled again.

Again, though unease grew in his mind, he subdued it. "Told me what?"

"Your transfusion..." began the doctor.

"I'll tell him, Cail," interjected Melody. "It's my responsibility."

A cocky grin on his face, Melody's brother nodded at the clothing in Nick's lap. "You might want to get dressed."

Refusing to be intimidated by the superior look in the other man's eyes, Nick tossed the sheet aside, rose and dressed. If that silver-haired bastard thought Nick was uneasy about standing naked in front of the three of them, he had another thought coming. On more than one occasion, Nick had been forced to leave a place in various states of undress. Modesty didn't mean a hell of a lot when his life was on the line. "So," he said after he pulled a tee shirt over his head, "start explaining."

Melody's brother held out a piece of paper. "You better read this. The sheriff said you'd probably want to see it right away."

Snatching it from the other man's hand, Nick quickly scanned it then started. His assignment was terminated. Just like that. He could take some vacation time then report back to headquarters by the end of next month.

Black spots appeared behind his eyes.

He blinked them away.

"Nick?"

Crumpling the paper in his fist, he looked at Melody. "What do you have to explain," he glanced at the doctor, "besides how a cut that drained at least three pints of blood from me has healed in a day and a half to the point that it looks more like a scratch?"

Melody chewed her lip. "Maybe you want to sit down?"

He crossed his arms over his chest. "I'm fine. Start talking."

She glanced first at her brother then the doctor. "Remember why you came here to begin with? You're looking for Jake Hurley?"

"I know why I'm here."

She chewed her lip. "Well, I know you're really looking for him because he's supposed to be a werewolf."

For a few seconds, Nick just stared at her. How did she know? His mission was top secret. "That sounds pretty farfetched."

A nervous smiled played about the corners of her mouth. "Not really. You see, he actually is."

As Nick stared at her, his stomach rolled again. More black spots danced before his eyes. "Is what?"

"A werewolf. And his name isn't Jake Hurley. It's Garth. Garth Gray. He's my brother."

"The one who handcuffs women to his bed?" Nick

snapped out. He had to say something.

"No, Eileen would never allow that."

"Eileen?"

"His mate…er, wife."

Nick shifted his weight. "So, if Jake Hurley really is a werewolf and is also your brother, that makes you a werewolf too. Who are you trying to kid? Do you think I'm nuts?"

She shook her head again. "Since you received a pint of my blood…"

Nick snorted. "I'm a werewolf, too?"

"Not exactly. You can't shift into wolf form, but your senses are much better than they were before. You can see, hear, and especially smell much better. You are stronger and can run faster and longer. And you heal faster. That's why your wound is so much better in such a short time."

Smirking, Nick looked at the two other men in the room. "Since you're her brother, that makes you a werewolf. How about you, Doc? You a doggie too?"

Still grinning a superior grin, Melody's brother said, "I told you he wouldn't believe you. Do you want to show him or should I?"

After a long sigh, Melody said, "I'll do it."

As Nick watched, a silver mist manifested around Melody and her clothing fell to the ground. Thin at first, the mist became thicker, swirled faster. Then as quickly as it formed, it disappeared. In Melody's place—on top of her clothing—sat a silvery-white wolf.

Stomach rolling, Nick stepped back. More and more black spots began to dance before his eyes. A loud roaring in his ears blocked all other sound.

The silver mist appeared again. In moments, Melody stood before him—completely dressed.

Nick grabbed the back of a chair to steady himself. "That was a neat trick."

"I can do it too if you'd like. So can the doc—except for the clothes," Melody's brother said in a cocky voice. He turned to his sister and added, "I'm impressed, Mel. I thought Dad was the only one in the family who could morph in and out of clothing."

"I've been practicing," was her answer. Then, "Nick, are you okay?"

Their voices seemed to come from a great distance.

Heart thudding in his chest, Nick tried to fit what he just witnessed into the reality he believed in. Werewolves didn't exist. They couldn't. If they did, and Melody was one, then he'd had sex with a…

The roaring in his ears grew louder. His stomach rolled and heaved. The spots before his eyes blurred into a black mist.

From somewhere deep inside of him, a dark, dangerous voice said, *I'm free!*

As the black mist folded itself around Nick, Melody leaped forward, only to be pulled back as both her brother and Cail grabbed an arm.

"What's happening to him?"

"Damned if I know," the doctor stated. "If anything, humans get nauseous from the initial transfusion. That's it."

He'd no sooner finished speaking than the mist dissipated. Tangled in Nick's clothing, a lean, wide-eyed, black wolf, tongue lolling out as he panted heavily, stared up at them with golden, black-flecked eyes. In an instant, the mist reformed and disappeared. Nick reappeared before them on his hands and knees, his clothing still tangled around him.

Staggering to his feet, his still golden eyes wild with fear and rage, he shouted, "What the fuck did you people do to me?"

Chapter Thirteen

ꙮ

Leaping past Melody, Nick lunged for the door and disappeared through it.

Melody started after him only to be brought up short when her brother grabbed her arm.

"Mel, let him go."

Nostrils flaring, Melody glared into her brother's eyes. Her words were sharp and succinct. "Let. Me. Go."

He didn't let her go. If anything, he held her more tightly. "Melody, he's not what we think. He shouldn't have been able to shift."

"All the more reason for me to go after him."

"You could get hurt."

"He is my mate. He will not hurt me."

"Damn it, Melody, he doesn't understand what that means. Did you see his eyes? They were yellow! They should have returned to their normal color. The *Were* blood has done something to him. There's more to this Nick Price than we understand. He's not human!"

"Neither am I! Now, let me go before I chew off your hand!"

"Let her go, Brendan," Cail interjected. "The transfusion has affected him strangely, but he's completely disoriented by the change. Melody is a powerful *Were* in her own right. She'll be able to avoid any real danger from him."

Wrenching herself free of her brother's grasp, Melody bolted out the door after Nick.

Raking the fingers of both hands through his hair as the door slammed behind his sister, Brendan turned back to the doctor, who was now pulling a slim book out of the bottom drawer of an old cabinet pushed against the wall.

"What the hell is going on, Doctor? You said Price was human."

The doctor shook his head as he paged through the book. "I said he wasn't *Were* but just assumed he was completely human. I checked his blood myself for any trace of *Were* before I gave him the transfusion, but I didn't look for anything else since I had to get blood back into him fast. I did notice something strange about his monocytes, but he'd lost so much blood I didn't have time to study them as much as I wanted. After all, what are the odds he'd be anything but human?"

Brendan leaned closer. "What are you looking for?"

The doctor didn't answer but kept flipping pages. Then he stopped and slid his finger down the page until it came to rest beneath a black-spotted, horseshoe shaped figure. "Damn."

"What?" Brendan asked.

The doctor stared at the paragraph below the picture. "Vodun."

"What?"

The doctor looked up. "Your sister's mate is a direct descendant of a true voodoo priest or priestess, close enough that the magic of the voodoo combined with *Were* blood has given him the ability to shift. His reaction tells me he either didn't know or doesn't believe. I doubt if there's any danger for Melody."

"That's easy for you to say," Brendan growled. "She isn't your sister."

Stopping short on the sidewalk, Melody looked both right and left.

Nick was nowhere to be seen.

"You lookin' for that black CIA fella?" an old man called from across the street.

Melody focused on the pair of cronies sitting in front of the hardware store whittling on a couple pieces of wood. "Which way did he go, Hank?"

"He high-tailed it down the street to his truck faster than a jackrabbit bein' chased by a coyote. Never did see anybody run so fast."

"He told me he was a sprinter in college," Melody called back as she started in the direction of the saloon at a sedate pace. Hank and his pal were human. Seeing one person running faster than anyone should be able to could be explained away with an excuse like she'd just used. If she sprinted after Nick, seeing two people run faster than was normal would have Hank asking too many questions. Her vehicle had been parked at the saloon, too. Hopefully, Nick was headed for his motel instead of straight out of town. She needed to talk to him, to explain what was happening.

Ten minutes later, she pulled into the empty motel parking place next to Nick's truck. Sucking in a deep breath, she momentarily rested her forehead on the steering wheel. Nick's transformation had been a shock. Somehow she had to make him understand…

Melody raised her head and stared at herself in the rearview mirror. Understand what? If she were in his place, would she react any differently? But what choice had she had? He'd needed blood.

But not necessarily yours, her conscience whispered. *Cail could have gotten more blood from some other human for Nick. He didn't need your blood to survive.*

He is my mate! snarled the werewolf in her soul. *He is mine!*

"Oh shit," Melody muttered to her reflection. "Now I'm having a three-way argument with myself." Pushing the door open, she slid out of her vehicle and sniffed the air. Nick's scent led to the motel door in front of his parked truck.

After one more deep breath, she strode to the door, grabbed the doorknob, and turned it. To her surprise, it opened. He hadn't locked it. Then again, considering his state of mind, that wasn't surprising.

Pushing the door open, she stepped in.

The lights were off and the heavy drapes were drawn. Except for the light coming through the door with her, the room was pitch black.

The click of a bullet clip being shoved into a pistol echoed in the small room.

"Put your hands up before I blow your head off."

Nostrils flared, she swiveled her head to catch Nick's scent and find him in the dark room. Nevertheless, she raised her hands. "It's me, Melody."

"I could smell you when you opened the door." His voice was bitter.

She swallowed. "Please, Nick, let me explain."

"Explain how you turned me into a freak?"

The anger in his voice wrenched her heart. What if he wouldn't understand? "You're no more freak than I am."

"My point exactly."

"Nick..."

The hand holding the gun didn't waver. "Shut up and listen. You wanted to save your brother. I can understand that. But turning me into a freak was going too far, Melody Gray. Give me one good reason why I shouldn't shoot you now."

Melody felt her anger gathering. "I didn't give you my blood to save my brother. I gave you my blood to save your life because you're my mate."

"What the fuck does that mean?"

She smiled a weak smile she didn't even know if he could

see. "It's basically the same as being married."

Melody winced at his snort of disgust. "You've known me less than a week, fucked me twice, and decided to marry me—without asking if I was interested?"

Melody fought to control her anger. "It doesn't work like that! Wolves know when they meet their true mates. As soon as I looked in your eyes, the wolf half of my soul went crazy. *You* are my soul mate, and, and if you look deeply enough inside of yourself, you'll know I'm telling the truth."

He laid the gun on the dresser and stepped toward her. "Give me a fucking break. Sure, you're good in bed, but I'm not marrying any woman I've only known a couple of days, especially one as weird as you. Now get out of here."

She shook her head. "No. Not until you understand what's happening to you."

Hands on his hips, he leaned forward. "Oh, I understand what's happening to me all right."

Melody shook her head again as she fought her inner wolf, which wanted to leap into Nick's arms. "No, you don't. You have to guard yourself, your identity even more closely now. You can't let humans get any of your blood. Not only would you be in danger, but you'd be risking the lives of thousands of others. Please, Nick…"

Anger continued to rumble through his voice. "Why didn't you think of that before you did this to me? That fax your brother gave me was a recall. This case is closed. Your brother would have been safe without you screwing up my life."

She stamped her foot. Why did he have to be so obstinate! "Damn it! This is not about my brother. He could have killed you at least ten times in the last couple of years."

He crossed his arms over his chest. "He could have tried."

She fisted her hands on her hips. "No, asshole. He would have killed you and left your body to rot in the middle of nowhere."

"So why didn't he? It would have saved him a lot of aggravation."

Melody stomped closer. "Because, you idiot, he works for the CIA too. He knows exactly what the reaction would have been—send more agents to find out what happened to you. Instead he chose to run and hide, never staying long in one place, never being able to settle down and live a normal life until..."

"Until? What changed?"

"He found his mate."

He threw up his hands. "Christ. Not this fucking mate bullshit again."

"It's not bullshit," she snarled through gritted teeth. Why oh why did this bull-headed, argumentative, thick-headed *human* have to be her mate? She wanted more than anything to wipe the sneer off his face—then jump his bones and screw him until neither one of them could walk.

"Cut the crap about the mate shit, Melody. You've got a great imagination, I'll give you that, but I figured you out that night we played pool. You're a spoiled WASP princess who was born with a silver spoon in your mouth, even if you are pretending to rough it right now. I did a background check on you. Your dad is a hotshot perfume designer who owns a company with stock that keeps increasing in value. You're slumming it right now, and when you saw me, you decided to see if there was any truth to those rumors about black men."

She gaped then snapped her mouth shut. "Truth about black men?"

"Yeah, whether or not our cocks are bigger."

Melody didn't restrain herself. She was too angry. Leaping across the room, she wrapped her hand around his throat, and slammed him against the wall. "You fucking asshole! You don't know shit. WASP princess? Me?"

Momentarily stunned as speckles of bright light danced

around his head, Nick nevertheless quickly gathered his senses. Melody had moved far more quickly than he'd anticipated. Fucking werewolf blood. Gathering his strength, he grabbed her upper arms, spun them both around and plastered his body against hers so that she was now the one trapped against the wall.

She didn't fight him, and the light coming through the open door illuminated the tears that rolled silently down her cheeks. "Let me tell you just how much of a WASP princess I am, Nick Price of the fucking CIA. I was born deep in the Rocky Mountains in a cave overlooking an uninhabited valley. I wasn't even a year old when my mother was shot—dead. My father became deeply depressed. The only things that kept him going were my sister, my brothers and me, and it was pretty obvious to us that once we could take care of ourselves, he'd take his own life."

Shock coursed through Nick's body. Was this the truth? "Why didn't he go to the police? Your mother was murdered."

"Police! We wouldn't have gotten any help from them. My mother was a wolf! My littermates and I made Dad teach us to shift. As human children, we'd need him a lot longer than we would as wolves. Our plan worked. Dad took us to live with a pack of werewolves. Do you know what that was like? Human minorities, no matter where they're from, aren't the only ones who deal with prejudice and racism. Most of the other *Weres* looked down on us because Mother was a full wolf. We were ridiculed, snubbed, belittled. If Dad hadn't been as powerful as he was, our lives would have been worse. It wasn't until he formulated his cologne and we moved to New York that our lives got better."

It was Nick's turn to gape then gather his composure. "Your mother was a wolf? A real wolf? I had sex with a..."

"A *woman*, you idiot," Melody snarled. "A woman who enjoyed it very much—just like you did." Leaning forward, she pressed her mouth against his.

Unprepared for her attack, Nick froze. When she slid her

tongue along his lips, he automatically opened his mouth. Her sigh filled his mouth followed quickly by her tongue as she tilted her head to the side and moved her lips slowly over his.

Deep in his soul, *something* roared to life. Releasing her upper arms, he trailed his hands down her sides to her waist as he slid a thigh between hers. As their tongues danced together, his cock thickened and hardened. She lifted her arms and wrapped them around his neck. He slid his hands from her waist to her ass where he cupped her buttocks and pulled her hips against his. She rubbed her crotch against his thigh, and he could feel her nipples digging into his chest. As their kiss went on, her scent surrounded him, the scent of roses, woman and arousal. He sucked her tongue further into his mouth. The urge to rip off her clothing and bury his cock deep into her was almost overpowering—almost.

Realizing what he was doing, Nick pulled his mouth from hers. Melody Gray was the hottest woman he'd ever been with. He had to admit that. But that didn't mean he couldn't resist her if he wanted to. And he wanted to. She was not important to him. She *would not be* important to him. He would walk away from her without a second thought.

"Nick?"

Her eyes were clouded with passion—and promise.

Nick tore himself out of her arms. "Leave. Now! I… Just get away from me. I need to go home."

Confusion appeared on her face, and she shuddered. "Nick…"

Spinning away from her, he pounded his fist on the dresser at his side. A crack splintered its way across the top. "Damn it, Melody. Leave me alone!"

She sucked in a deep breath then moved to the door. When she reached it, she turned around. "I'll leave for now, Nick. But you need me as much as I need you. As much as you may fight against me and whether you believe it or not, I'm the only woman in the world who can make you happy. That kiss we just shared proved it. You're mine, Nick, and I'm yours. You can't fight fate." Turning, she stepped out the door and disappeared. The sound of her vehicle starting and leaving rolled through the door.

Nick lifted his head and gazed at his reflection. There was enough light to see the black flecks floating in his now-golden eyes. Melody was wrong. She had to be. She wasn't the only woman who could make him happy. Once he was home, he'd prove it to himself and her. Aunt Jasmine would help him figure out how to deal with this—this *change*. There had to be something that he could do to get his life back to normal.

Chapter Fourteen

ꟗ

Go back! Mate! My mate!

Clenching her teeth, Melody turned off the highway and onto the dirt road that led to her cabin. Her wolf half had been raging at her since she'd walked out of Nick's motel room. But Melody was her father's daughter. She could and would control her *Were* blood. As she drove over the last hill, Melody bit off a curse and she parked next to her brother's SUV. He *would* have to come to her cabin.

He was waiting outside on the porch.

The breeze rolling down off the mountain swirled around the flower baskets hanging from the eaves of her porch and carried the light scent of the flowers she had planted in them to her. She ignored it. "What do you want?"

"I'm sorry, Mel."

Of all the possible things her brother Brendan could have said to her, sympathy was the last thing Melody expected. She blinked as tears welled in her eyes. "Nick said he's going home. I have no idea where that is. What am I going to do, Brendan?"

Brendan held up a manila folder. "I think I know."

Plucking it from his hand as she walked by, Melody disabled the security system then unlocked her front door. Once inside, she pulled the few sheets of paper from the folder and read them. "Vodun?"

"Voodoo," her brother answered from behind her.

"Voodoo? What does religion have to do with Nick being able to shift?"

Brendan walked past her and flopped down onto her

sofa. Leaning forward, he rested his elbows on his knees and clasped his hands. "It's not just a religion. Some priests and priestesses have magic, some very powerful magic. Your doctor says Nick must be a close relative to one. Mixing your *Were* blood with the magic in his has given him the power to shift. The doctor also thinks he didn't know about it since he was so shocked."

"And how does this help me find out where he is?"

"Think, Mel. I know you don't want to ask Dad for help. You're a good detective. What city in this country is most likely to have practitioners of voodoo?"

She stared into his eyes. "New Orleans."

"Exactly. Nick may not be from the city itself, but he's undoubtedly from Louisiana, and New Orleans has a *Were* pack."

Melody nodded. "I'll be leaving in the morning."

"Leaving? Why don't you give him some time to think?"

Melody shook her head. "He's my mate, Brendan. My wolf half is raging at me for walking away from him in the first place. If I don't go, I'll go crazy. Someday you'll understand."

Brendan snorted. "Like hell. That's one misery I can do without."

Melody couldn't help the small smile that appeared on her face. "You won't have much choice when Ms. Right comes along. One look in her eyes and you'll be lost. Take my word for it. You think I'd have picked the CIA spook chasing Garth?"

Wearing his familiar grin, Brendan rose and chucked her under the chin. "Good luck finding him. Just give me a call if you need any help."

Stepping back, Melody slapped his hand away. "How many times do I have to tell you not to do that. Belle may tolerate your irritating habits, but I won't. Next time, you'll lose that hand."

Her brother simply grinned and pulled her into a tight hug. "I have to get back to New York. Dad's sending me to England in a few months so I've got things to arrange. Don't forget about the family gathering at Belle's. You don't show up, and the entire family will come looking for you. We don't want Dad tearing around New Orleans. The pack Alpha down there probably wouldn't be too thrilled about it."

Melody sniffed. "Dad could probably take him with one hand tied behind his back."

"Yeah, probably, but that would sure screw things up politically with him being a Hierarchy member now. You know how conservative the ruling body of werewolves is. Besides, what would he do as Alpha of the New Orleans Pack? He doesn't have time to lead it."

Another smiled forced its way onto Melody's lips. "You could always do it. The responsibility would be good for you."

Brendan's snort widened her smile. "Like hell! Do you know how hot and humid it is down there during the summer? And swamps are not good wolf habitat."

Melody nodded as the smile left her face. "I'll try to make it to Belle's, but if I can't find Nick..."

"You'll find him. You're a good PI. Put your skills to use." After another hug, he headed for the door. When he reached it, he stopped and turned. "Remember, if you need me, just call."

"I will. Be careful driving."

He tossed her his usual reckless grin. "I'm always careful." He pulled the door closed behind him.

Outside, Brendan slid into his vehicle, started and backed it up, and headed for the highway. Once he was over the hill and out of sight of Melody's cabin, he stopped and pulled out his cell phone. Melody was very resilient and capable, but she was headed into a very large pack's territory, a pack that, in the past, had been known for attacking uninvited *Weres*. Supposedly, the new Alpha was cleaning house and dragging his pack into the twenty-first century, but Brendan wasn't going to take any chances. He didn't have any contacts in New Orleans, but his father did. Melody had no idea just how much more power her father had accumulated since his appointment to the Hierarchy.

Thirty miles away and deep in the verdant forest, the sheriff pulled a naked Kenny out of his four-by-four, unlocked his handcuffs, and shoved the younger man. "Get going, and don't come back."

"You can't do this to me!"

"Be glad the Pack, including your mother, voted to banish you instead of execute you. You put all of us in danger with your unwelcome advances on Melody. You presented your suit. She said no. That's all there is to it."

"She's going to be my mate. I want her!"

"Christ but you're more thick-headed and stubborn than a mule. Shift and leave. Maybe living in the *Wilde* for a while will straighten you out." He drew his revolver and pointed it at Kenny. "Now git!"

"You'll regret this, Sheriff. You all will. Just wait."

"Don't come back, Kenny. You won't get off so easy."

Spitting curses at the sheriff and rest of the pack, Kenny shifted and loped away.

Shaking his head, the sheriff got into his vehicle and headed back to town. That boy was going to come to a bad end. He just knew it.

Half an hour later, Kenny rounded a bend in the path he was following only to come to a skidding halt. Before him sat a huge wolf.

Relief swept through Kenny.

Forest Brother. I ask for aid.

For what?

My pack has banished me and taken away my mate.

The Laws of the Pack do not allow that—unless you were challenged for her.

No, I wasn't. I have been treated unfairly.

I challenge you.

Kenny backed away. *What?*

The female Were *you want, whom you attacked, is to be my mate. You have no right to her. You have no right to harm her.*

What? Who? How do you know?

A fox heard from an owl of the Were *who threatened the silver-furred female. She is mine.*

The fight was brutal but short.

Licking the blood from his jowls, Drake trotted away from the other wolf, who now lay whimpering beneath a dead pine tree. He should have killed the young upstart, but he had fought so pathetically, Drake had refrained from ripping his throat out. The youngster had sworn to leave the area and never return. In Drake's opinion, the wounds he'd given the young *Were* and his promise never to return were sufficient. Besides, Drake had made one thing perfectly clear. If the young *Were* returned, he *would* kill him.

Grabbing his bag, Nick hurried across the airport terminal to the counter where he could rent a car. In another hour, he'd be home. One of Aunt Jasmine's mint juleps—or three or four or five—would go a long way toward helping him relax. The entire flight had been one of the worst he'd ever experienced. His newly enhanced sense of smell had bombarded him with scents he'd never noticed before. He'd never realized that so many women—and men—wore too much perfume or cologne that sometimes didn't mix well with their natural scents. Luckily, none of those had been sitting near him. The air in a plane was far more stale than he'd realized, and the seats could use a good cleaning. Most shocking was the fact that he'd recognized two women on the flight with him as werewolves. And judging from their reactions, they'd believed him to be a werewolf too. The elder had nodded stiffly while the younger had curled her lip in a silent snarl. Again, thankfully, their seats hadn't been near his.

But he'd had a lot to think about during the flight, about how his life was completely screwed up thanks to Melody Gray and her stupid idea that she was his mate. Christ, what the hell was he supposed to do now? The only thing keeping Nick sane was the knowledge that somehow, someway, Aunt Jasmine would be able to help him.

The key to his rental in his hand, Nick hurried through the terminal, more scents bombarding his newly sensitive nose. One strange, eerie scent brought him up short, and he locked gazes with a tall, pale man standing in a shadowy corner. The man flashed a toothy grin, nodded once, then sauntered away.

Nick simply stared. What the fuck was he? He wasn't human and he wasn't werewolf. A thought exploded in his mind. Vampire? Vampire! They were real? Holy shit, what else was real? Everything from nightmares and fairy tales?

Sweat broke out on Nick's forehead as he hurried forward. He had to get out of here, had to get home.

His emotions in turmoil and completely distracted by what had happened to him, Nick never noticed the two men who fell in behind him. Retrieving his car, he left the airport. A dark sedan followed him.

In the shadowy corner, the man Nick had correctly identified as a vampire spoke into his cell phone in a low voice. "A man fitting the description of this Nick Price just arrived and rented a car. Do you need anything else?" He listened for a moment then grinned. "You are more than welcome, Artemis. Anything you need, just call me."

Chapter Fifteen

ꟃ

The booming thunder seemed to shake the car and howling winds tossed leaves and branches at his vehicle as Nick drove down the long, muddy road. Both the wind and thunder fit his mood perfectly. Cursing as muddy water along with bits of rock and gravel splashed up onto his windshield from a particularly deep rut, he wrenched the steering wheel to the left only to plow through another muddy puddle. A slender branch covered with green leaves bounced off the hood as he swung around the final turn and pulled to a stop next to his aunt's neat, white house. Turning off the ignition, he leaned his forehead against his fists as they clenched the steering wheel. How had his life become so fucked up? What did he expect Aunt Jasmine to do about it? Why had he even come home? Hell, he'd turned into a fucking wolf! What if it happened again and he attacked her? If he ever hurt his aunt, he'd never forgive himself. Better for him to leave before Jasmine knew he was here.

Lifting his head, he reached for the key.

As he did so, the door to the house was flung open and his aunt, ignoring the wind and rain, stepped out onto the porch. The look of pure joy on her dark, unlined face was too much for him, and Nick sighed. He could no sooner leave now than he could stop breathing. Eyes closed, he sucked in a huge breath and reached for the door handle.

"Who dat?" she asked with the customary New Orleans greeting when he stepped onto the veranda, then continued with the traditional endearment for a beloved child even though he was almost thirty, "Boo!" Not waiting for an answer and unmindful of the raindrops dripping from him, she walked into his embrace and wrapped her arms around him.

The top of her head barely reached his chin as she laid it against his chest.

He grunted as she squeezed him.

"It's so good to have you here." Pushing herself free of his embrace, she turned, grabbed his wrist and tugged him through the door. "Come in, come in. Get out of dat rain. I just put on water for coffee, good coffee, not dat weak water dat's suppose to be coffee up north. I baked pralines this mornin', and I have jambalaya simmerin'. Or if you want somethin' quick, I can make you a po-boy."

As his aunt rambled on about food, Nick followed her into the kitchen and allowed the homey scents to envelop him. The spicy aroma of the jambalaya tickled his nose while the underlying fragrance from the morning's baking teased his memory with the remembered sweetness of his aunt's pralines. The soft melodies of his aunt's New Orleans accent calmed him, and, for the first time in twenty-four hours, a sense that she would be able to fix everything like she had when he was a child blossomed in his heart.

Across the room, his aunt's large orange tomcat was draped over one of the kitchen chairs. As soon as Nick stepped inside, he opened his eyes, lifted his head, and sniffed. Flaring his nostrils, he sniffed again. Instantly, his eyes widened. Leaping from the chair, the cat simultaneously puffed out his fur and hissed. The words *wolf* and *flee* exploded in Nick's brain as the cat catapulted across the floor and into his aunt's snug sitting room where it disappeared beneath the fringed cloth that covered a small table.

Nick gaped in the direction the cat had taken. "He talks? Your cat can *talk*?"

His aunt gaped back at him. "You heard him?"

Nick locked gazes with his aunt. Before he could comment, she scurried across the floor and cupped his face in her hands. "What happened to you?"

"What are you talking about?"

"Your eyes."

Clasping her wrists gently, he pulled her hands away, strode into her sitting room, stopped before the mirror hanging on the wall, and stared at his reflection. Eyes with yellow irises containing black flecks stared back at him. The hope the sound of his aunt's voice had kindled sputtered and died.

His aunt grasped his upper arm and pulled him around. "Nicholas, what's been done to you?"

Sighing, he sank into a chair and buried his face in his hands. After a few seconds he lifted his head and stared at his aunt. "I lost some blood and needed a transfusion. I got it from a werewolf." Sliding from the chair, he fell to his knees in front of her, wrapped his arms around her, and buried his face in her waist. His muffled voice drifted upward. "Aunt Jasmine, I turned into a wolf. What am I going to do?"

Cupping the sides of his face, she lifted his head and looked deeply into his eyes. "Tell me everything."

Fifteen minutes later, Nick leaned back in his chair and stared at his aunt. He had told her everything—well, almost everything. She really didn't need to know about the wild sex he'd had with Melody.

Lips pursed, she stared back. "I never heard of this happening before—not with the Vodun, but when the fairy folk mix with us, their power is enhanced. Must be the same with de *Were*." She cupped his face in her hands again. "But which power is taking you? Me, I never heard of any Vodun shifting to wolf before."

Pulling away from her comforting hands, Nick closed his eyes. There really were fairies. There were probably trolls, ogres and unicorns, too. Opening his eyes again, he asked with a sigh, "It's all true, isn't it? Everything I've heard about Voodoo—sticking pins in dolls and devil worship."

Snorting, she shook her head. "Bah! Most of those stories

are for tourists and Hollywood movies. The truth about Vodun is what you hear from me. It can be good magic, healing magic of the Earth."

"Loa," Nick said. "I remember you telling me bedtime stories about the Loa, when I was small."

Smiling with approval, his aunt nodded her head. "The good spirits God sent to watch over the Earth. Everything has its Loa."

"Yeah, Loa, spirits, whatever." He stared deeply into her eyes. "What about me? What am I supposed to do? Aunt Jasmine, I turned into a freaking wolf!"

"He been in dere 'bout half an hour, André," the first watcher said to the man who'd just joined him and his companion next to their car. The Spanish moss hanging from a large oak tree shielded them from the house. Thankfully, the rain had stopped.

André frowned and wiped the sweat from his brow. The quick thunderstorm had passed and the thick humidity was back. "Why would a strange *Were* come to Mama Jasmine? How would he even know how to find her?"

Both his companions shrugged. "Mais, don' know me. We follow him like we do all de strange *Weres*," said the second.

André stepped forward through the moss. "Only one way to find out." He reached the veranda in moments.

"Damn it, Aunt Jasmine! I don't want to be a wolf!" rolled out through the screen-covered windows. "You can fix it, can't you? Can't you cast a spell or ask a Loa to fix me?"

André stopped short. Jasmine Vassant only had one nephew that André knew of, the one who worked for the government, and he was human. How had he become *Were*? Stepping up onto the veranda that wrapped around the house, he knocked on the door.

Inside, the conversation stopped. In seconds, Jasmine appeared at the door.

The brief flicker of surprise that flashed in her eyes was quickly masked. "*Bienvenue* André, *entrez*. Your *expertise* is needed," she said in a tight voice.

"*Merci,*" André answered as dipped he his head but kept the grimace from his face. Mama Jasmine would not appreciate the fact that her nephew had been followed here, and André, for one, was not in the habit of angering such a powerful Vodun. Though she did not condone using the black arts, she was more than capable of conjuring an uncomfortable *gris-gris* on him. Following her into her house, André sat in the chair she indicated and stared at the younger man who stood across the room. His nostrils flared once, and the corner of his mouth lifted in a silent snarl. The strong scent of *Were* emanating from him was unmistakable. How the hell had that happened?

"André, my nephew Nicholas," Jasmine said, "Nicholas, this is André Bayon, Alpha of the New Orleans *Were* Pack."

"I can smell him," Nick snarled. Just what he needed, another werewolf to fuck around with him.

His aunt was across the room in a flash. Standing before him, she stared up into his face and snapped, "André is a guest in my house." She shot a sour glance at the lithe *Were* who had the grace to look somewhat abashed. "Even if he came without an invitation. You will treat him with the respect and dignity his position merits, or you will leave."

Before Nick could answer, the *Were* rose and bowed slightly. "My sincerest apologies, Mama Jasmine. My men had orders to follow any strange *Were* who did not seek out the Pack. I did not know they followed your nephew." He cocked an eyebrow. "I did not know he was *Were*."

"How much did you hear?" Jasmine asked.

"Only that he doesn't want to be *Were*. How did it happen? Blood transfusion?"

Jasmine nodded. "Is there any other way?"

Across the room, Nick watched the Alpha carefully. Then he grimaced. He wasn't reading the Alpha by sight, he was *smelling* the Alpha's reactions. The *Were*'s scent had become stronger after his aunt's question. Nick leaned forward slightly. Obviously, the Alpha didn't want to answer his aunt's question.

The Alpha looked into Nick's eyes and cocked an eyebrow.

Nick crossed his arms over his chest and glared back. He didn't give a damn about any secrets the Alpha didn't want to divulge.

"There are," the other man finally answered, "but they aren't important if a transfusion is what turned him."

"Can it be reversed?"

As soon as the question left his mouth, a mental picture of Melody walking away from him appeared in Nick's brain. His stomach clenched and he broke into a cold sweat. Melody leave him?

Gritting his teeth, he forced the image away. So what. She was just another woman—and a freaky one at that. The further away from her he could stay the better. He turned his attention back to the other man.

"It's final."

His aunt shook her head. "How can you be sure? You've only been Alpha for two years."

Rising, André scowled. "I don't ask you about your secrets, Mama Jasmine. Don't ask me about mine. I am Alpha. I know what I know."

Fists clenched, Nick stepped forward. Alpha or not, this guy needed an attitude adjustment. However, before Nick was able to take more than two steps, an acrid scent slashed through the still air and invaded the room. A sense of darkness enveloped Nick and that *something* that was coiled around his insides like a snake ready to strike stirred again.

Chapter Sixteen

ꟸ

Across the room the Alpha's nostrils also flared as he jerked to a tense alertness.

Nick's aunt looked from one man to another. "What is it?"

The sound of steps on gravel had her scurrying to the screened sliding door that opened onto the veranda. "Who dat?" she called.

As the footsteps drew nearer, the foul odor wafting into the room became more pronounced—excitement and fanaticism heavily mixed with malevolence. Nick hurried to his aunt's side. Whoever this person was, he was dangerous. When André stepped to his aunt's other side, the feeling of relief that surged through Nick's body was followed quickly by irritation. He didn't need anyone to help him protect his aunt, much less a mangy werewolf. He had little time, however, to dwell on those thoughts. Instead he leveled his full attention on the tall, muscular, black man who stepped onto his aunt's veranda.

The man's white teeth sparkling, he smirked at Nick's aunt and said, "Mama Jasmine, where ya't?"

Instead of the usual "Awright" used by many of New Orleans' inhabitants to greet someone, she answered, "Ya go backatown where ya belong."

Nick kept his expression blank. His aunt had slipped into the dialect she reserved for people she did not want to impress—or those she didn't want to know just how educated she was.

The black man never stopped smiling though his scent became more acrid. "Now, Mama Jasmine, ya know I been lookin' ta meet you nephew." When his fanatical gaze shifted, a chill slid down Nick's spine. At the same time, that *something* dark inside him stirred again.

"Mais, my Nick don' wanna talk to you, Manno Cousan."

"But I wanna talk ta him." Cousan switched his attention to the werewolf. "What ya doin' here, Bayon? You pretty far from yer pack. Didn' think ya had the balls ta go anywhere alone, yeah?"

The werewolf crossed his arms over his chest and looked at the heavier man. "Who says I'm alone, and I'm not the one Jasmine told to leave," he answered as three more men sauntered out from behind some bushes in the garden. The largest cracked his knuckles as he walked.

On the other side of Jasmine, Nick shifted his feet when a soggy breeze brought the scents of two other werewolves to him. When the Alpha glanced his way and nodded almost imperceptibly, Nick flared his nostrils in answer. Obviously, the Alpha counted Nick as one of them.

The tension became as thick as the humid air.

Nick's aunt was not about to allow a brawl on her veranda. Putting her hand on André's arm, she said, "You go on home, André. We talk again later."

Manno stepped closer. "Stay away from my people, cur. Dey ain' yer business." His three companions halted at the edge of the veranda.

Nick watched as André leaned forward, but his Aunt Jasmine's hand on the werewolf's arm stopped him. Without another word, André turned, walked back through the kitchen and disappeared out the door.

The scents of the other two werewolves vanished from the heavy air.

His aunt rounded on her other visitor. "Get out, Manno! *Passé*! You ain' welcome here."

The big man settled into one of the veranda's wicker chairs, stretched out his long legs and grinned an evil grin, his dark face emphasizing his white smile. "I am yer prince, Jasmine. You treat me with respect."

"Bah! You ain' no prince of mine. You ain' no prince of nobody. Go away before I put *gris-gris* on you."

Cousan simply grinned at her. "You won'. Foolish woman, you *afraid* to use you powers for anythin' other den *white* magic."

His pronunciation of *white* made it sound like a curse.

"My aunt told you to leave," Nick stated as he crossed his arms over his chest. "Do it."

The other man turned his attention to Nick. "I thought ya were goin' to let a woman talk for ya." Standing up, he rose to his full height so he could look down at Nick. "De time's come for ya to join me, Nicholas Price. Throw off de chains of da white man. Accept you royal Vodun blood. With the transfusion of *Were* blood, you more powerful dan any Vodun in ten generations—even you aunt. Join me, and with you connections in the government, we rule dis city, yeah."

"Why the hell would I want to rule the city?"

Manno stretched his arms wide. "Power, man. Power."

"You're fucking crazy."

Lowering his arms, Manno took an angry step toward Nick. "Fool, dat *Were* blood woke you Vodun half. Don' you feel it? Learn to use dat power, and you be invincible."

"I don't know what you're talking about," Nick scoffed.

The other man smiled. "I have power too. How do you think I know about you?"

"Power? Bullshit!" Nick sneered. "You probably bugged my aunt's house."

The slight widening of the other man's eyes told Nick he'd guessed correctly. "Get out, now," Nick growled. He took one step forward.

The three men crowded into the doorway and Manno smiled. "You will come wit me now, Nick Price. You have much to learn."

Letting a wicked smile slide onto his lips, Nick pulled out the semi-automatic revolver he'd slipped into the back waistband of his pants and pointed at the men. "I don't think so."

Even Cousan stepped back.

"Get out and don't come back."

The four men stared at the gun.

Nick's hand didn't waver. "I *will* use it. Who the fuck is going to question the actions of a government agent in a case like this, especially when you and your men probably have rap sheets a mile long?"

For a moment, fury blazed from Manno's eyes. Then, "Don' be a fool. Power surges through you veins, dark power. You need to learn to control it and Jasmine can' teach you. Da blackness will eat you from de inside out. Only I can teach you."

"Bullshit."

Shaking with anger, Manno leaned forward. "Fool! You won' deny me!"

The click when Nick released the safety on his revolver was audible across the veranda.

All three of his henchmen grabbed hold of Manno and pulled him off the veranda.

Nick didn't relax or lower his gun until they disappeared. Lifting his head, he sniffed. Cousan's acrid scent and the scents of his men were fading. As he clicked the safety back on and lowered the gun, the blackness struggling within his soul exploded in his head, and he crashed to the floor.

The sour odor of smelling salts brought Nick back to his senses. Sneezing violently—the *Were* blood amplified the pungent smell a hundred times—Nick pushed himself to his feet then pulled his aunt up from where she had been kneeling at his side and immediately began questioning her. "Who was that asshole and what royal blood was he talking about? It's bad enough I changed into a wolf. Now I have some Voodoo asshole chasing me around to help him conquer the world. What the hell is happening to me, Aunt Jasmine?"

For the first time in his life, Nick thought his aunt looked old. Sighing deeply, she set the smelling salts on a small table and turned toward the kitchen. "Come. We have coffee."

Once they were seated with mugs of thick coffee before them, his Aunt Jasmine cupped her hands around her mug and sighed.

Gulping hot coffee, Nick wrestled his emotions into a tight ball and locked them away in a corner of his mind. He had to think, to use his brain, to approach everything that was happening rationally. Christ, the government had spent thousands upon thousands of dollars training him not to panic and to think clearly in any situation—and he was one of the best agents the CIA had.

His thoughts now clear, Nick leaned back in his chair.

His aunt looked into his face. "Manno has no Vodun powers."

Before she could say anything else, Nick held up his finger in front of his lips while rising to his feet. After a quick trip to his car for a dark bag, he pulled out a small, black, box-like instrument. Flipping a switch, he canvassed every room in the house. In fifteen minutes, he'd discovered and destroyed four listening devices that had been carefully hidden. "Maybe now you'll let me install a security system," he said to his aunt.

Fire sparkling in her eyes, she slapped her hand on the table and glared out a window. "*Bracque*! Crazy! Manno Cousan goes too far. It is past time for the Council to do something about him."

Pulling her back to the table, Nick pushed her gently into her chair and poured her another cup of coffee. "Who is he?"

Her arm jerked as she slashed her hand through the air.

"He is nobody—a man of no family, but ten years ago, he came to New Orleans claiming to be a direct descendant of a Vodun royal house. Those of us who are Vodun knew immediately he wasn't, but he was charming and polite and treated us with respect." She hissed and gulped coffee. "He is a two-faced devil. Over the years he worked patiently but insidiously to undermine the true teachings of Vodun. Instead he preaches the Voodoo darkness as portrayed by the fools who make motion pictures as the way to great powers, powers he has promised to his followers. Worse, he's convinced a few true Vodun to join him. They've become corrupted by worshiping in the old, dark places in the swamps."

"Old Man Cyprus," Nick interjected as a dark memory from his childhood surfaced in his mind.

His aunt glanced up. "You remember. Almost, you died that day. An evil older then Vodun is Old Man Cyprus. Manno and his followers have dared to seek that power."

Nick was still lost in his memory. "I remember. That big gator…"

Aunt Jasmine nodded. "Saved you. He is a Loa, a protecting spirit."

Subduing his memory, Nick refocused his thoughts. "What does Cousan want?"

"He told you, power. He wants to rule like a king."

"So why does he want me?"

"He sees you as a way to dis power." She leaned toward him. "Those of us of the old bloodlines can learn to use true power, and power is like any tool. It can be used for good or evil." His aunt looked troubled. "Untrained Vodun often succumb to evil because the power is easier to manipulate and control—at first. Eventually, it will control the wielder. We do all we can to keep dat from happenin'. All descendants of a royal blood line are tested at a young age to see if dey be able to use the power. Many cannot and, even though you are a direct descendant, we could not wake the powers within you."

Jasmine gulped more coffee. "Your mother was also unable to use the power. She never told your father of your heritage. To him, Vodun was just the Voodoo tourists expect to see."

"That's why you never told me the truth," interjected Nick.

"Would you have believed me if I'd told you I could have turned that obnoxious Pierre Trousant who bullied you into a frog?" his aunt answered.

Nick smiled. "Maybe not, but I would have appreciated it at the time."

His aunt's smile was faint and fleeting. "The powers are awake in you now because of the infusion of werewolf blood, but I do not understand what exactly it's done to you." She frowned. "Your father, he used to say he was descended from the druids. Maybe that made the difference." She shrugged. "Who knows? But the werewolf blood has awakened your power in ways we were unable to foresee. Cousan will try to use you."

"Snowball's chance in hell."

"He is a dangerous man, Nicholas. Do not underestimate him."

Chapter Seventeen

ꟈ

Striding through the crowded airport, Melody readjusted the strap of her overnight bag and tightly clenched the keys to the car she'd just rented. Her flight to New Orleans had been uneventful, giving her lots of time to think long and hard about Nick Price and how he'd turned her life upside-down. As much as she wanted to hate him for changing her life, she couldn't. Her need for him precluded everything else. Now, all she had to do was find him.

The low snarl that erupted from deep in Melody's throat earned her stares from the people around her, but she ignored them. As she hurried through the crowd, she forced herself to acknowledge that she'd turned his life upside-down too, in a much more profound way. Worse, she'd given him her blood without his permission. True, his circumstances had been dire—he needed blood and the thunderstorm kept them from getting a helicopter to get him to a hospital or even bring blood in, but she'd gone against a long-standing tradition. She hadn't broken any of the Pack Laws, but still…

What would her father think?

Blinking, Melody chewed her lip. The longer she thought about it, the more she was able to acknowledge her actions had really been unconscionable. How could she have lost such control of herself? Why had she let the wolf in her soul dictate her actions? She'd known giving Nick the transfusion without his permission was wrong, yet she'd insisted on it anyway. The werewolf in her soul had completely subverted her will. She hadn't thought that was possible.

Melody stopped chewing her lip and gritted her teeth. It was done, and there was nothing she could do about it now.

All she could do was try to make Nick understand how important he was to her—how much she needed him. Sighing, Melody blinked back a tear. Never in her wildest dreams had she imagined she would need anyone as much as she needed Nick.

But finding Nick in New Orleans would be a long, time-consuming process—if she worked alone. Melody needed help and she knew just where to find it. She glanced at the sign pointing the way to the exit. Few humans would note the small symbols on the bottom, but to Melody they were as plain as the other words on the sign. As all werewolf packs did, the one in New Orleans had a compound. Directions to that compound were visible to anyone who knew where to look for them.

When she stepped outside, humidity blanketed her. As she wiped the perspiration from her brow, a slender man looked her way then nodded.

Shrugging out of her jacket, Melody nodded back. He was the third *Were* she'd seen. Obviously, the Alpha here kept track of any strangers who entered the city. Nor was she wearing the perfume her father had had specially formulated for her—the perfume that contained the aconite that masked her werewolf scent. No other *Weres* were able to detect her as long as she wore it. However, she didn't want to be incognito on this trip. If anyone would be able to help her find Nick, it would be the Pack Alpha of New Orleans. Considering how many *Weres* had been at the airport, Nick would have been marked as soon as he got off the plane. The Alpha here would either know exactly where Nick was or have a very good idea where Melody could look.

Once she retrieved her rental, Melody headed away from the airport and followed the covert signs that would lead her to the *Were* compound located just outside of New Orleans. An hour later, she pulled into a driveway that led to a locked gate. Eyeing the camera directed at her car, she pushed the button on the intercom. "Melody Gray to see the Alpha female."

When the gate swung open, Melody put her car into gear and drove up the driveway. Requesting to see the Alpha male would cause a stir among the Pack. A strange female *Were* visiting the Alpha female was far more common and less notable, and Melody wanted to stay as far under the radar as possible. All she wanted to do is find Nick, apologize for what she'd done, then convince him that they would be miserable without each other, and leave for home—preferably with Nick. The fewer people who knew she was here, the better.

Stopping in front of the stately antebellum mansion, Melody grabbed her jacket, got out of the car and gave the keys to the young man who'd opened the door for her. Without looking back, she followed an older *Were* inside the air-conditioned house where he led her to a small reception room.

"Madam will be with you in a moment." With those words, he bowed his head slightly and left the room—closing the door firmly behind him.

Laying her jacket over a chair, Melody smoothed her skirt, glad she'd worn one of the two tailored suits she owned, and wandered about the room to scrutinize the furnishings. She'd already noted the concealed camera in some intricate carvings on one wall of the room, which meant there were probably listening devices also. From what she'd learned of the New Orleans Pack from Brendan—he'd emailed all the information her father had on this particular Pack to her cell phone during her flight—the Alpha had only held his position for two years and was pulling what had to be the most insular and antisocial Pack in the United States into the twenty-first century. The Pack hadn't been all that cooperative, either. The current Alpha had had four challenges for the position in the first three months of his tenure, and had survived at least two assassination attempts. However, with the backing of his five loyal Betas, two brothers and three cousins, he was slowly but steadily making changes.

At the sound of the door opening, Melody spun around.

A dark-haired *Were* stepped into the room, perused her carefully, then left the room again. He returned shortly and held the door open for a very pregnant, petite, blonde woman. Judging from the air of total confidence and command that radiated from her, she was the Alpha Melody had come to see.

"Please send for tea, Jean-Pierre," she instructed the tall man with her. He stuck his head out the door, called softly down the corridor, then stationed himself right inside the door with a wary eye on Melody. Settling herself onto a settee as gracefully as she could, the woman turned her attention to Melody. "I am Noelle Bayon, Alpha female. *Bienvenue.* What can I do for you?"

Forgetting all of her intentions to be polite and civil, Melody strode across the room, stopped a few paces in front of her hostess, and answered, "I'm Melody Gray, and I want to know where my mate is."

As the man next to the door tensed and stepped forward, the woman arched an eyebrow. "If you cannot keep track of your own mate, why should I help you, Melody Gray? You are not of this Pack, though word of your arrival and your appearance has aroused interest in a number of our unmated males." She leaned back and stared into Melody's face for a moment. "However, I don't believe I can allow you to join us. You are Alpha to the bone, so would make my life very uncomfortable."

Hands resting on her hips, Melody leaned forward—which elicited a warning growl from the male who was much closer to them now—and answered, "I am *not* interested in any of the males in your pack. I want *nothing* to do with your pack. I just want to find my mate. He's here in New Orleans somewhere, and with the number of watchers you have at the airport, you know he's arrived and probably know where he is at this moment. Just tell me where, and you'll never see me again."

Completely unruffled, the smaller woman smiled up at her. "Again, why should I? I have more things to worry about than a strange female who's lost her mate—a strange female whose manners make me question her upbringing. Even the wolves in the *Wilde* teach their cubs better manners."

Silently cursing her own temper, Melody glared at the woman who still smiled slightly. She knew Melody would not attack. Not that Melody cared about the tall male guarding the Alpha. She was absolutely sure she could disable him without too much trouble. However, the Alpha female's pregnancy precluded any kind of physical altercation. The Second Law of the Pack was very clear. Cubs and pregnant females were to be nurtured and protected above all else.

Melody cursed herself silently. Why had she approached this female so antagonistically? She had always been able to control herself! If she'd have come into this meeting more rational, like she planned, she wouldn't have to resort to her final ultimatum. Damn Nick Price for messing with her emotions! But—she had to find him. Not knowing where he was, was tearing her soul in two.

Taking a deep breath, Melody spit an apology out. "I'm sorry. I don't mean to be so—demanding."

The smile never left the Alpha's lips. "Then you'd better learn to control your temper. If I weren't so—indisposed, I'd teach you some better manners myself."

That veiled threat was too much for Melody. Before she could stop herself, she allowed a slight sneer to tug at the corners of her mouth. "As I said, I am Melody Gray. My father is Artemis Gray. Unless you want him arriving at your front door, I suggest you be a bit more cooperative."

Only the slight widening of the woman's eyes betrayed her consternation at Melody's words. Before she could answer, however, the door opened and another man with a strong resemblance to the one already in the room walked in carrying a large tray on which sat an ornate silver service.

"You can leave us, *mon frére,*" he said. "We will be just fine, yeah."

"She de daughter of Artemis Gray," his brother growled.

"So I heard. It does not matter, for I have the information she seeks. Go check with Alain. He will brief you on matters from this morning."

The other man nodded and left the room as the Alpha—the confidence and air of command radiating from this second man left no doubt as to who he was—set the heavy tray he carried so effortlessly on the coffee table, turned his back on Melody, and leaned over and kissed his wife. "You've had an interesting morning, *ma coeur*?"

She accepted his kiss and the caress he slid across her large stomach with a smile. "Quite. We have an important guest."

Melody—and her werewolf soul—were in no mood for a polite *téte-é-téte.* This man knew where Nick was.

"Where is he?" Melody blurted.

Turning, the Alpha smiled at her.

"I would like to present my husband, André Bayon, Alpha of our pack," interjected Noelle.

"Tell me where Nick is."

Again, Noelle arched an eyebrow then snapped. "Really, I would think the daughter of Artemis Gray would have better manners. To first threaten us with his possible arrival and then make demands with no attempt at civility is unconscionable. Why should we help you? If you truly are his daughter and your mother truly a wolf, how can the powerful wolf soul you have permit such deplorable behavior on your part?"

Swallowing a growl, Melody clenched her fists, closed her eyes, and inhaled a deep breath. Shame flowed through her body. The woman was right. She was acting atrociously. The way she was behaving, her father would be more likely to support Noelle Bayon against her. And her mother…

Melody sighed. Her mother was probably rolling over in her grave because of her daughter's horrible manners.

My mate! Find him! Go to him! her soul snarled in her mind. So much for the manners of her wolf half. Melody struggled to maintain control. Her bond with Nick was just too new and too fragile. She'd been away from him too long.

Opening her eyes, she swallowed another growl and said, "You're right. My mother… Forgive me. I'm sorry. Nick and I, we've only been mated a few days. The strain of not being with him… The wolf in me…"

The Alpha female's anger dissipated quickly as she frowned. "You have not cemented your bond with a true mating?"

Melody shook her head.

She nodded. "Ah, that explains much. To be separated so early isn't easy. How could you let him go, how could he stand to leave, without the wolf mating? You need to calm yourself. Sit, have tea. My André will not allow your Nick to leave."

Melody smiled a lopsided smile. "You don't know Nick."

The Alpha poured tea and handed a cup to his wife. "Nick Price is at the home of his aunt. He will not be leaving for a few days, at least."

Joy flared in Melody's soul. *My mate! Go now!*

"You're sure?" She couldn't keep the eagerness from her voice as she reached for her suit jacket.

The Alpha nodded as he stared at Melody. "Are you sure you want to go now? Nick Price is an angry young man. He needs to learn about the changes he's undergone. His aunt is the only one he trusts."

"I have to go explain…" Melody stopped. Obviously the Alpha knew what had been done to Nick. Still, she didn't need to explain the guilt she felt for what she'd done to them. "Will you give me directions to his aunt's home?" After a moment, Melody added, "Please?"

"She will not be able to calm herself until she sees him, André. You remember how it was?" Noelle said with a smile.

He chuckled as he pulled a small tablet and a pen from inside his suit jacket. After a quick scribble, he handed it to Melody. "I've included directions with the address. You should be there in forty-five minutes."

"Thank you." Grabbing her jacket, she headed for the door.

"Are you sure you don't want some tea?"

The door slammed shut on Melody's "No thank you."

An hour and a half later—the Alpha's directions hadn't been as clear as he'd thought—Melody braked to a stop next to Nick's aunt's house. At least she hoped it was Nick's aunt's house. Pushing open the door, she stepped out. Thick humidity wrapped itself around her, and she wiped beads of sweat from her brow. Cursing the fact that she'd donned pantyhose for the flight, she clasped the front of her blouse and pulled it away from her clammy body. How would she ever get used to this humidity if Nick wanted to live in New Orleans?

That thought stopped Melody in her tracks. If Nick wanted to live here? Why should she live where Nick wanted? Why shouldn't he live where she wanted? She didn't want to live here!

She shook her head. Why was she even thinking about it? Is this what being mated did to a person? Ridiculous!

Clenching her fists and taking a deep breath, Melody stomped up the two steps to the veranda and knocked sharply on the front door.

Joy sang in her soul when Nick appeared. *My mate!*

Inside the screen door, he stepped back. "You? How did you find me? What the hell do you want? Haven't you screwed my life up enough?"

Melody could not control the longing in voice. "Nick, I—"

He slammed the door shut in her face.

Her heart in her stomach, Melody stared at the door. She'd expected his anger but not outright rejection. Was that possible? Didn't their bond affect him the same way it did her? What if he really didn't care? What would she do? She couldn't live without him. Of that she was absolutely sure.

She lifted her hand to knock again just as the door was opened. However, instead of Nick, she was greeted by an elegant black woman. Far shorter than Melody, the woman lifted her delicate chin and stared at Melody with dark, brown eyes. Her rich, red lips were drawn into a stern line and her voice was cool. "According to Nicholas, you have ruined his life. Why should I welcome you into my home?"

Melody blinked at the power radiating from Nick's aunt, power to rival that of her father. For once, the werewolf part of her soul was quiet. That allowed Melody to relax and give herself a chance to think before she spoke. There was something in the woman's eyes that belied the ominous tone of her voice—something that inspired hope. Could this woman become an ally?

She looked deep into the shorter woman's eyes and said, "Because without him, I'll die."

Before the words were even out, Melody knew they were true. The link her soul had with Nick was irrevocable and unbreakable. The single drawback of the bond shared by mated werewolves was the lack of interest in living with the loss of a mate. Unlike her father, she didn't have any children to pull her out of the melancholy that would overtake her if she was separated from Nick too long—or if he refused her. Instances of *Weres* refused by soul mates were almost unheard of—almost. Whispers of a *Were* pining to death or committing suicide surfaced from time to time.

Melody felt a single tear roll down her cheek. She blinked and swallowed the rest.

At the same time, her stomach growled. She hadn't eaten

a thing in the last thirty-six hours.

The other woman's face softened, and the power she'd wrapped around herself like armor dissipated. "I am Jasmine Vassant." She stepped back. "*Bienvenue,* Melody. *Entrez.*"

Stumbling through the doorway, Melody entered a room swirling with tantalizing scents—something spicy bubbling on a pot on the stove, something sweet piled in a container on the counter, and something hot, male and sexy sitting on the other side of the room—Nick.

"A woman, a stranger, just drove up to de house and went inside."

On the other end of the connection, Manno grinned. "*Mais,* she *Were*?"

"Paul says she is."

Manno grinned even more broadly. Subverting a few of the New Orleans' *Were* population to his beliefs had been a great stroke of luck. Not a *Were* entered or left the city without him knowing about it. "She be de one who give him de *Were* blood. No reason for any other *Were* to come after him."

"What we do?"

Manno's smile became decidedly wicked. "Take her if she leaves. You know where. If it is true what Paul told us about mated werewolves, we will be able to use her to control him."

Chapter Eighteen

ℌ

As Melody stumbled across the threshold into his aunt's kitchen, Nick slapped a hand onto the table. "Aunt Jasmine!"

"Mind your manners, chile! This is my house, and this woman is welcome—for the moment. You want to find out what happened to you. Who better to explain?"

Nick swung his gaze from one woman's face to the other. His Aunt Jasmine he trusted and loved more than anyone else on Earth. Melody…

Melody he didn't trust, did he? Just how did he feel about her?

Clenching his fists, he continued to stare into the face of the woman who'd ruined his life. Right now he was more pissed off than he could ever remember being with anyone, including his asshole boss who'd sent him on this wild goose chase to track down a werewolf. Now look at him. He was a freak, and if the CIA ever found out, they'd lock him up and do experiments on *him*! Melody had been right about that. If he'd ever been able to drag her brother back to Washington, he'd have been locked up tighter than Fort Knox.

Melody! Fucking bitch. What was he supposed to do about her? More than anything, Nick wanted to walk away. He *would* walk away. If Jasmine didn't ask her to leave, then he himself would. He didn't want to be anywhere near her. Yet…

When he gathered his will to command his body to rise, his stomach clenched. Sweat beaded on his forehead. Black spots appeared before his eyes. As much as he wanted to march across the kitchen and right out the door, he couldn't. *Something* wouldn't let him. But what? Damn it! He'd spent years learning to control his emotions and body. For the last five years, he'd been totally dispassionate during every job he'd been on. All that had changed since Melody Gray had given him her blood.

No, said the insidious voice of his conscience. *You haven't been completely dispassionate with this case since the first time you saw her sitting exhausted at her desk. You have lied to yourself ever since that day. Why else didn't you just leave once you got the information she gave you? You knew it was false, but you could have picked up the trail without her. Instead you stayed—because of her. You stayed and watched as she masturbated in her bedroom. You followed her into that bar. Why did you challenge her to the pool game you knew you couldn't win? When she grabbed your wrist, why did you let her pull you into the alley behind the bar? And when she had you strapped down on that hospital bed, you didn't fight her with more than a few words. All that happened before you knew about the transfusion. Admit it. Be honest with yourself. You wanted to have sex with her.*

"Fuck!" Nick blurted out as he wrapped his fingers around the back of a chair.

"Nicholas!" his aunt protested simultaneously with the crack of breaking wood.

He stared down at the piece of chair in his hand.

"You're stronger than you were before," Melody said in a small voice. "Considering your training, you'll have to be careful."

Slamming the smooth wood to the floor, Nick growled, "I don't want to be stronger."

"Now you sound like a petulant child," Jasmine said in stern voice. "What's done is done. Stop poutin'."

"I am not—"

"Yes you are, dawlin'." His aunt turned to Melody. "Is the change permanent?"

Melody lowered her eyes and nodded. "I'm sorry…"

Nick stomped toward her. "You're *sorry*! *You're* sorry? How the hell do you think I feel? According to you, I'll never have a normal life now. I was perfectly happy with things the way they were, but you took it upon yourself to change all that, didn't you? You've ruined my life."

By the time he was finished shouting, Nick was standing right in front of Melody. She stood with her head bowed and he could have sworn he saw a tear drop to the floor.

Her obvious misery had no effect. "Bitch!" he snarled.

That did it. Nostrils flaring, Melody clenched her fists at her sides to keep from slapping the sneer off his face and raised her head. Enough was enough. She'd followed this man hundreds of miles because her soul cried out for him. But, she wasn't about to be browbeaten by him even if he was more important to her than anything else on earth. She was *Were*, and no female allowed her mate to treat her with anything except respect. She'd leave scars on his hide before that happened.

"That's right," she snarled back. "I *am* a bitch. My *mother* was a bitch, and so was every other female relative of mine, and I'm *proud* of it. You toss that particular word around like it's derogatory, but to me or any other female *Were* it's a simple statement of fact." Unclenching her right fist, she jabbed her finger into his chest. "And as for ruining *your* life, what the hell do you think you've done to mine? I was perfectly happy with my life until you strutted into my office like you owned the place. Do you think I wanted to be mated to you—a human? Do you think I would have chosen you?" She jabbed his chest again, and he stepped back. "Think again, idiot. I wanted to mate another *Were*, someone who would understand me and love me for who I am. But who does my wolf soul pick? You—a human."

Another jab to his chest and another step forward for Melody. "Do you have any idea what it's like to have your insides twisting into to knots because your mate isn't close by? Do you know how it feels to have your mate leave you without a word of goodbye? Can you even begin to understand how it feels to see your mate lying in a pool of blood in danger of dying? Damn it! I didn't have a choice. What did you expect me to do, let you bleed to death?" She jabbed him with her finger again.

Nick stopped backing up and leaned toward her. "You didn't have to give me *your* blood, especially when you knew what it would do to me. Did you ever hear of free choice?"

Fisting both hands on her hips, Melody stomped her foot. "Haven't you been listening to me? You are my mate, the other half of my soul. You were dying. I panicked."

"Panicked? You seemed to be in pretty good control of yourself before that."

She leaned in to him until their noses were almost touching. "You weren't *dying* then, damn it! Werewolf blood would heal you faster than anything else. It's been three days and you barely notice a wound that should still have you stretched out in a hospital bed, right? No, I didn't give you a choice. I was wrong, and I'm sorry. But I never had a choice either. The bond between us was too new. I couldn't control it. I still can't."

Melody jerked her head back, raised her chin and stared directly into his eyes. "And you have no idea how much I hate that."

Nick glared back at her. She raised her finger to poke him in his chest one more time, but he grabbed her hand before she was able to make contact. He'd had enough of her jabs and was putting an end to them right now.

The moment Nick enveloped her hand with his, however, what felt like electrical shocks danced around their hands and up his arm. His stomach rolled and that *dark something* in his soul surged. This time, though, something different was happening to his body. His stomach rolled again and his heart began to beat faster. Sweat broke out on his forehead. As the darkness gathered behind his eyes, something *else* tangled around it, struggled with it, fought with it. His stomach rolled one more time then tightened into a hard knot.

Panting, Nick closed his eyes. His entire body started to shake.

"Nick?" Pulling her hand free, she cupped his face with her palms. "Are you okay?"

Opening his eyes, Nick stared into her face, stared into her deep, blue eyes, blue eyes that sparkled with golden flecks. He had to kiss her, no, needed to kiss her. His very life depended on it. Before she had a chance to deny him, Nick pulled Melody into his arms and captured her mouth with his. As her scent surrounded him, joy erupted in his body, and the ugly, evil darkness that struggled to control his body disappeared.

Slanting his head, Nick pressed his mouth more firmly against hers and slid his tongue between her lips. Their teeth clicked and clashed. His kiss wasn't gentle, but he couldn't help himself. He needed to get her as close to him as possible. If he could have, he would have swallowed her whole. Growling low in his throat, he sucked on her lower lip then thrust his tongue back into her mouth.

As he parried his tongue with hers, she moaned and pressed herself more tightly against his torso. With that small victory, he seized control, his kisses drawing forth a hungry, burning response. He invaded her mouth, thrusting and swirling his tongue against hers in a dance that became more and more sensuous. He needed to conquer her, to dominate her.

Keeping one arm around her waist he laced the fingers of his other hand through her hair and pulled her head even closer.

Again teeth clashed against teeth and tongues stabbed and swiped.

Her teeth slid across his lip.

The metallic taste of blood rolled across Nick's tongue. His absolute need for Melody intensified as a bonfire ignited in his veins. Trapped in a kiss that seemed to drag his soul from his body, Nick plummeted into a maelstrom of desire.

She slid her hands up his back then back down to massage his ass cheeks through his jeans. She tried to say something, but with their tongues in each other's mouths, he couldn't understand a word.

It didn't matter. Her actions spoke much louder. The tight knot in his stomach exploded with fiery heat. As his nerves sizzled, his cock hardened. Moaning deep in his throat, he slid his hand down her back, cupped her butt, and pulled her hips against the hard ridge of his erection.

She was his!

Whimpering, she ground herself against his thigh then cradled his erection between hers.

Gasping, she pulled her mouth from his and threw back her head.

"Yes," she hissed.

He wanted to rip her clothing off, lay her down on the floor and make her his then and there.

The sound of his Aunt Jasmine clearing her throat—very loudly, more than once—permeated the fog of passion surrounding Nick's brain. Thrusting Melody out of his arms, he stumbled back. Gasping for breath, he stared first at her then at his aunt.

Her eyes glazed with passion, Melody grabbed a chair to keep from falling. "What..."

Without a word, Nick turned and fled deeper into the house. He'd never experienced anything like the feelings coursing through his body. He had to get away from Melody, had to get somewhere he could think without her distracting presence.

Mine! Mine! Mine! Mate now! howled Melody's soul as she staggered to regain her balance. "Nick!"

"Let him go, chile," Nick's aunt said as Melody took a

step after him. She laid a hand on Melody's arm only to snatch it back when Melody turned and snarled.

Stepping back, she held up both hands. "Peace, chile. He needs to think. He's not runnin' away."

Sucking in deep breaths of air, Melody stared at Nick's aunt and struggled to regain control of her body. The kiss she'd just shared with Nick had been like no kiss she'd ever had before, even those with him. This one had drawn the soul from her body, melded it to his, and returned parts of both. He truly was her mate, and now she was his.

She raked her hair back over her forehead. Now all he had to do was acknowledge her and not fight what couldn't be changed.

"Something important just happened, didn't it?" his aunt asked.

Melody nodded. "We're linked. I'm part of him now whether he likes it or not. I don't know exactly what the transfusion did to him or what part his Vodun blood plays, but he is my mate. I have no doubt, and if he'll just stop fighting with himself, he'll know it too."

Jasmine shook her head. "My Nicholas, he's used to controlling his own life." Lifting a tightly sealed container, she held it out to Melody.

"What's that?"

"My jambalaya. Your supper. Go get a room at the closest motel and stay dere tonight."

"I'm not leaving my mate."

Nick's aunt tsked. "Go on, girl. Nick isn't going anywhere, but he don't want to see you right now. He has to sort this out in his brain for himself." She held the container out. "Here. Go eat, get a good night's rest and come back in the morning."

Melody raked her hair back again. She had her restless soul under control now and could think. Maybe Nick's aunt was right.

Her stomach growled as the tantalizing aroma of the jambalaya on the stove drifted around the kitchen. She grimaced when Jasmine smiled.

Melody sighed. The memory of the final look of shock and disbelief on Nick's face surfaced in her mind. Jasmine was right. Nick needed time to think, to acknowledge and accept what had happened.

Taking the container of jambalaya, Melody turned toward the kitchen door. "I'll be back tomorrow morning."

Jasmine nodded. "I'll make sure Nick is here waiting for you."

Once outside, Melody slid into her rented car and placed the container on the floor between the two seats. Pulling the keys from her pocket, she started the car and backed away from the house. Driving slowly down Jasmine's long driveway, she pulled her cell phone from the bag she'd left on the front seat and punched in her sister's number.

Belle answered almost immediately.

"Belle, I found him. We talked, sort of. I think his aunt is going to help me."

Melody stomped her foot onto the brake. "Oh shit." Then, into the phone, "There's a tree down. I'll have to get out and move it. Don't worry, it's just a small tree. Don't hang up, I'll be right back."

Melody laid her phone on the passenger seat and opened the car door.

She'd barely stepped out when hands grabbed her.

Her snarl was audible through the phone connection to her sister. "Who the hell are you? Let go of me. What do you—"

Melody didn't have a chance to finish. A rag soaked in some foul liquid was shoved over her mouth and nose. In less than a minute, she was unconscious.

On the other end of the line, Belle gaped at the phone in her hand. Then she quickly severed the connection and punched in another number.

"Melody's been kidnapped."

Chapter Nineteen

"Open you eyes. I know you awake."

Chin resting against her chest and hair falling over her face, Melody ignored the command.

The hard slap that snapped her head to the side was completely at odds with the soft voice.

"Don' screw wit me, bitch."

Jerking her head back so she flung her hair away from her face, Melody stared up into the man's face. "Don't screw with me, asshole. You have no idea who you're messing with."

He grinned at her. "What? I supposed to be scared jus' 'cause you *Were*? Jus' 'cause you have da pointy teeth?" He snapped his fingers. "Dis what I think of da Pack."

"You are an idiot," she snarled.

Hands on hips, he threw back his head and laughed.

Melody heard the door open, but she kept her attention focused on the man in front of her. Her nose told her he was human. How did he know about the *Were*, and what did he want with her? How could he be fool enough to kidnap her if he knew about the Pack here in New Orleans? Even though she wasn't a member, the Alphas here would do everything in their power to protect any *Were* from non-*Were*. Different Packs and individuals may argue amongst themselves, but they always united against anyone who wasn't *Were*.

The man who'd opened the door joined him.

Keeping her attention on her tormentor, Melody ignored the room's new inhabitant. *He* was *Were*. What was going on here? Was the local Pack behind her kidnapping? She snarled, "Who are you and what do you want with me? I'm not from

New Orleans. You certainly aren't going to get anything for me from the Pack here."

The first man laughed again and thumped his chest with his fist. "I Manno Cousan, Vodun King of New Orleans. Da Pack? I don' want nothin' from dem. Dey don' have nothin' I want. Dey worthless to me." He lifted Melody's backpack from the floor and swung it to the other man. "Here, see what you find out, Jacques."

The *Were* grinned at her as he grabbed the swinging pack and stepped over to a table where he dumped everything out. Pushing the few pieces of clothing aside, he grabbed her wallet. "Her name Melody Gray." He frowned for a quick second then shrugged. Dropping her wallet, he picked up her cell phone. "Dis pretty expensive technology for jus anybody, Manno." He flipped it open and punched some buttons as Manno stepped to his side. "Anythin'?"

"Jus' a bunch first names." He dropped the phone and continued to look through her belongings.

Manno returned to stand before her. "Who are you? Why you have a phone so expensive? You family have lots of money? Dey pay to get you back?"

A very loud howl from the other man caught both their attentions.

"What?

"Abomination!" Jacques howled as he waved a piece of paper in his hand. "She Abomination!"

Manno stepped to his side again. "What you mean?"

"Artemis Gray! She de cub of Artemis Gray."

"What you mean, abomination? Her mama her papa's sister or somethin'?"

"Worse! Artemis Gray, he a *Were* who went feral and mated a wolf."

Manno shrugged. "De *Were* do dat. De Pack don' care."

"He supposed to stay wolf. He din'. He taught his cubs to

shift, taught dem to be *human*! She half wolf. She *more* wolf den human! She supposed ta stay in da woods wit da other *animals*!" He spat on the floor at her feet. "Abomination!"

Smiling slightly, Melody stared at her captors. It had been a long time since another *Were* castigated her parentage to her face. Her father had become too powerful. Still some *Were* had trouble coming to terms with her family. Not many half-*Were* wolf pups chose to become human and, if they did, they lived very low profile lives. Her father, on the other hand, seemed to have gone out of his way to elicit controversy. Of course, his purpose was logical and honorable—equality for all *Were*.

"You really half wolf?" Manno asked. "Nick Price know dat?"

She switched her attention back to the human. Nick? What did this Manno Cousan want with Nick? "That's none of your business."

"She din' tell him," Jacques growled. "You voodoo prince been fuckin' an animal."

Melody kept her eyes on her captors, but her mind was whirling. Nick was a voodoo prince?

"Vodun, fool, Vodun!" Manno snapped. "Voodoo for tourists. Vodun is real. You know dat!"

Jacques bowed his head slightly. "It her fault. I don' want ta be in da same room wit her."

"By all means, leave," Melody interjected. "I'm not enjoying your company either."

A backhand from Manno snapped her head to the side again. "Shut up, bitch."

Licking the blood from the corner of her mouth, Melody struggled to control her temper as her werewolf soul howled in anger. *Tear out his throat!* The urge to shift became almost overwhelming—almost.

Manno laughed at her. "Go 'head. Shift, bitch. Wit you legs tied to da chair, and you arms behind you, you dislocate you hips and shoulders. An' you still be tied up. Jacques, here, he likes to watch de pain. Maybe he untie you den and fuck you."

"Wouldn' fuck her if she da last *Were* on Earth. I don' fuck no animals."

Manno chuckled and rubbed his crotch. "Maybe I try her later. Do it doggy style."

Sweat popping out on her forehead, Melody ground her teeth together and concentrated on controlling her raging inner wolf. She tested her bonds slightly. They were tight. But she didn't think shifting out of them would be impossible. It would take all her skill, though, and there was the chance she could fail. To attain her wolf form still bound would completely disable her and cause excruciating pain. Best not to attempt it unless she had no other option. Slowly, the wolf inside her accepted her decision and quieted.

Completely under control again, Melody looked into her captor's eyes and said, "You still haven't told me what you want from me."

Obviously disappointed, Manno shrugged. "I don' want nothin' from you. You da bait for Nick Price. You woke his powers when you gave him you blood. He a powerful Vodun now. Me and him, we gonna rule dis town, maybe even da state, maybe even da country."

Melody blinked. Nick? Rule the country? "You're truly an idiot if you think Nick wants to rule anything—especially with you!"

This time, his slap was hard enough to topple the chair onto its side. Tiny bits of light sparkled before her eyes as her head smacked against the cement floor.

"Let her lay there, Jacques. She need to learn a lesson. Da message sent to Mama Jasmine's house?"

The other man nodded. "Nick Price want to see his wolf bitch again, he gotta come here."

Manno grinned down at Melody. "I get Nick away from dat *cooyon* aunt and talk ta him man to man, he see my side.

Every man want to rule, yeah." He turned to Jacques. "Watch her. Make sure she don' do nothin' stupid."

"As long as I don' need to touch her."

As Manno left the room, Jacques settled himself into an old lounge chair with the stuffing falling out and turned on a small television. After one last glance in her direction, he completely ignored Melody.

Lying on her side, still tied to the chair, Melody examined as much of the room as she could—cement floor, cinder block walls, empty boxes and pallets lying about. Some kind of warehouse, probably.

Closing her eyes, she inhaled deeply. The throbbing in her head became a dull ache. After another deep breath, Melody began reciting a favorite yoga mantra silently. Until the pain went away, she would not be able to concentrate well enough to shift herself out of this predicament. Looked like she'd have to wait for Nick to come and get her.

She gritted her teeth at that. Damn but she hated the idea of having to rely on anyone. She'd always been able to take care of herself.

Challenge! The word darted through every room of the New Orleans Pack's mansion, rocketed to every corner of the large estate.

Questions flew from one Pack member to another.

Again? Another one? Who? Wasn't everyone satisfied? Surely André had defeated every other male in New Orleans who coveted his position. There hadn't been a challenge in almost a year. The Desmaries brothers had been soundly defeated, Jean Dupaul had died of his wounds, and Henri Girard had fled the city after he lost his challenge.

Inside the mansion's ballroom where he'd gone when he'd been informed a strange male Alpha had forced his way past the gate guards with little trouble, André stood facing the wide double doors in the opposite wall. Behind him, her hands folded on her large belly, Noelle shifted nervously from one foot to the other. In her condition, she would be unable to help him.

Nodding to various Pack members as they hurried into the large room, André waited for his adversary.

In far less time than he'd expected—his challenger must have sprinted up the long driveway—the doors André was staring at were thrown open. A tall but lean, silvered-haired male strode across the room. Power mixed with the scent of exhaustion rolled off the strange male.

Behind André, Noelle gasped.

André didn't have time to turn and comfort her. A few more steps and the strange male would be halfway across the room—the traditional spot for him to stop and declare his challenge. Then, both of them would strip and shift. The fight would last until one of them accepted defeat, something André would never do. By the looks of this male, he wouldn't either. André swallowed once and locked eyes with his opponent. He was absolutely sure one of them would die in this fight.

But why would he challenge André when he was so obviously tired and not at his best?

Gasps echoed around the room when the strange male didn't stop the traditional distance from André. This was an unprecedented breech of protocol.

Noelle snarled and stepped to André's side.

Grabbing her wrist, André pushed his mate back behind him.

Other members of the Pack shifted their feet. Some took a few steps forward.

André's three cousins came to stand at his back. By breaking protocol, this strange *Were* had brought about his own downfall.

The stranger, red-eyed and haggard, ignored everyone except André. Stopping a few paces in front of the Pack Alpha, he leaned forward and snarled, "Where the fuck is my sister?"

Chapter Twenty

"What do you want?" Nick growled through the screen door at the scruffy man who stomped up onto his aunt's porch. When he pulled his revolver from the back waistband of his pants and pointed it at the stranger, the man stopped abruptly.

"Manno he says to give you dis, yeah," he said as he tossed a backpack onto the porch. "He says Mama Jasmine, she know where Manno at." With those words, he spun on his heel and trudged away.

Nick kept his gun in his hand until the other man's scent faded completely away.

"What is it?" his aunt asked.

Nick didn't have to get any closer than he already was to know. Melody's scent was all over it. Pushing the door open, he stepped out and lifted it. "It's Melody's."

His aunt sucked in a breath and frowned. "Manno has her?" She placed her hand on his arm. "Nick, he will kill her if he doesn' get what he wants."

Eyes unfocused, Nick stared out through the screen door. Songs from numerous birds rippled through the trees. Somewhere in the swamp, a bull alligator bellowed. Bees buzzed among the flowers and herbs surrounding the house. His aunt's cat yowled with frustration as the mouse he was stalking escaped his pounce. The morning breeze brought myriad scents to him—flowers, insects, animals. The sun, promising another hot, humid day, shone brightly. Not ten minutes ago, those sounds and scents had been a balm, soothing the tenseness from his muscles, the tiredness from his spirit, the confusion from his brain.

He'd spent the night tossing and turning, running the last week through his mind. First he'd berated himself for even meeting Melody Gray. He hadn't needed to stop in her town. He should have kept right on going. That train of thought, however, hadn't gotten him anywhere. He never ignored a lead, no matter how small. More than once, something seemingly insignificant had led to an arrest, and he was nothing if not thorough. He could not have refrained from approaching Melody Gray for information any more than he could have stopped breathing. Everything that had happened afterwards was as much his doing as hers. The fact that she was a werewolf, even though he hadn't known it, really had nothing to do with the attraction he'd felt for her. He had wanted her naked and moaning underneath him from the first instant he'd seen her sitting exhausted behind her desk. He just hadn't been willing to admit it to himself, to admit he'd finally found something more important than whatever case he happened to be working on.

Nick shook his head. Melody had fascinated him from the first and the fact that she was a werewolf didn't dampen that fascination. In the darkest hours of the morning before the sun rose, Nick finally admitted to himself that her being a werewolf made her even more appealing to him. Why, he didn't know. He should be appalled or disgusted, but he wasn't.

An owl hooting outside of his window had agreed with him.

As the red dawn broke, Nick finally accepted the fact that Melody meant far more to him than his own life, and the thought of never seeing her again roused depression and agony in his soul such as he'd never experienced before. He couldn't live without her if he wanted to.

His aunt's voice penetrated his thoughts.

"Nick?"

Nick shook his head to clear it, to focus his thoughts. His aunt's voice disappeared as did the sounds and scents swirling around her home.

Melody was in danger. Manno Cousan had kidnapped her.

Nick clenched the strap of Melody's backpack more tightly.

Her scent and that of the perfume she wore rose to embrace him.

Something inside Nick stirred. The brightness of the sun faded to black and something dark and dangerous stirred inside of him.

Manno Cousan was going to die.

"I'll kill him for this," he growled as he dropped the backpack to the floor. "Tell me where I can find him."

An hour later, Nick and his aunt parked on a deserted street. On the other side stood what looked like a dilapidated warehouse.

"Are you sure she's here?"

Jasmine nodded. "Dis is where Manno comes for his 'conjurings'," she answered.

"Stay here," Nick commanded as he slid out of the car.

Jasmine watched as Nick crossed the street and disappeared around the corner of the building. Settling her brightly patterned shawl around her shoulders, she got out of the vehicle and strode across the street. While Nick had been retrieving weapons from the arsenal he had hidden at her house, she'd made a phone call. The word would spread. Manno Cousan had finally gone too far. The Council would deal with him today. Stopping beneath a high window, she cocked her head to the side as she waved her fingers. Then she tucked her hands inside her shawl to wait.

On the other side of the building in an equally deserted alley, André and Brendan exited a nondescript van followed by five of André's pack.

"You're sure Melody's here?" Brendan growled. The sooner he got his teeth on this Cousan, the sooner the bastard's blood would run red.

The Alpha nodded to his companion. "This is where Cousan tries to perform his so-called magic. One of my pack, he infiltrated his organization."

"Let's go." Silvery mist began to form around Brendan.

The Alpha grabbed his arm. "Wait! Someone comes."

Brendan resisted the urge to bite off his host's hand. As much as he'd rather be here by himself, protocol had demanded that he accept the Alpha's offer of help. Brendan's father had been very adamant about that. The Hierarchy couldn't afford a blood feud between one of its members and the Alpha of the New Orleans' Pack. So Brendan tolerated the presence of André Bayon and his men for his father's sake.

A single figure slid through the shadows around the building's corner.

Brendan lifted his head and sniffed. More anger erupted in him. This man was the reason his sister had been kidnapped. His sneer became a growl. "It's your fault she's here. If she's been hurt, I'll rip out your throat."

Remaining flat against the building, Nick mentally cursed when he recognized Melody's brother. Then he growled back. "Don't move. There's a camera not ten feet from you. A few more steps and you'll be in plain view of whoever's in the building."

The Alpha shook his head. "It matters not, *mon ami*. Cousan, he knows we're coming."

"Manno knows I'm coming," Nick snapped back. "Did he send you a message asking for your company?"

"If you think I'm going to stay out here while my sister is in there, you're crazy," Brendan snarled in a low voice.

Nick felt like punching Melody's brother. Brendan's basic

strategy of a frontal attack sucked big-time. Nick stepped in front of him and stared into his face. "I'm not telling you to stay out here, cocksucker. I'm telling you to wait until I get their attention. They're only expecting me. Get the fuck over behind those crates before that camera swings this way."

Growling audibly when the Alpha grabbed his arm, Melody's brother still allowed himself to be pulled away. "If anything happens to Melody," he snarled, "I'll kill you myself."

"I'd like to see you try," Nick snarled back. He turned his attention to André. "There's a broken window around the corner. I didn't spot any cameras there. You'll have to boost someone up, but it's your best point of entrance without being seen. The cameras around the building are state of the art, but whoever installed them left gaps. You should be able to get in without any problems." He glanced back at Brendan. "And keep that asshole quiet."

Melody's brother curled his lip at him but didn't say anything.

I guess he's not totally stupid, Nick thought to himself. Then he slipped out of the shadows and stepped into the line of the camera. As he'd expected, it zeroed right in on him. After staring into it for a few moments, he walked directly to the door. A buzzer sounded and he heard the lock snap. Shoving the door open, he stepped into the shadows.

"I'd like to rip his throat out," Brendan rumbled to no one in particular as they slid quietly around the corner of the building in search of the window Nick had mentioned.

"Then, Brendan Gray, you will have to explain yourself to your sister," André drawled. "Mais, she didn't impress me as the forgiving type."

As one of the men boosted him to the broken window, Brendan snarled but didn't answer. Brother or not, Melody would rip strips out of his hide if he harmed one hair on the head of her mate. That still didn't mean Brendan had to like him. Because of that asshole CIA man, Melody's life was in danger. And if she was hurt in any way, Brendan wouldn't have to worry about taking revenge on anyone. His father would see to that.

Inside the warehouse, Nick remained still until his eyes adjusted. His enhanced olfactory powers quickly identified the scents of mold, dust, spoiling food, blocked sewers and unwashed bodies. The faint odor of Melody's perfume emanated from a door about forty feet in front of him. However, he'd spent his life using his eyes rather than his nose. In a situation like this, he preferred to rely on the sense he knew best.

"Why you fuck her?" a voice in the shadows off to his left said. "Her mama pure wolf—not *Were*! She more animal den human. What's wrong with you? Didn' you know?"

Nick didn't flinch when the *Were* stepped into his line of sight, though he wanted to strangle the life out of the other man because of what he had said about Melody. He had known the other man would be there, would have known he was there without enhanced senses. This was the type of job he'd been trained to do. Nick felt a cynical sneer curl his lip. Manno Cousan didn't stand a chance against him. And if this self-styled Voodoo king had hurt Melody in any way, he wouldn't live to see the sun set.

The man held out his hand. "You gimme yer gun."

Nick handed over the pistol tucked into the back of his pants.

"*Mais*, how you stand fuckin' dat bitch?" the other man continued as he shoved the gun into his belt and turned away. "Don' you know she Abomination? She half wolf. She half animal! You didn' know, did you? Get rid of her, man. Better, kill her. No one will know. "

What a fool. He never searched me for any other weapons.

"Shut your mouth before I shut it for you," Nick snapped.

At first, the other man caressed the pistol butt. He looked like he might accept Nick's challenge. Then, after staring into Nick's eyes for a minute, he backed away. Spinning on his heel, he walked forward, grumbling under his breath. Nick heard him repeat "Abomination" more than once.

For a few brief seconds, shame rose in Nick. He'd called Melody a privileged princess who'd been born with a silver spoon in her mouth, someone who only wanted to fuck him because he was black. She'd told him he was wrong, that her life hadn't been easy, but part of him hadn't really believed her. Now he knew she hadn't been lying about how she and her siblings had been treated. The *Were* he followed now hated her simply because of her parentage. He wanted her dead!

Nick growled softly, and the man looked over his shoulder. Nick glared at him. This man would die if he had so much as touched her.

He remained silent as the *Were* led him through the door he'd noticed before. They entered a well-lit room.

"Mais, you come," Manno said, satisfaction dripping like venom from his voice.

Ignoring him, Nick concentrated on Melody where she sat handcuffed to a chair in the middle of the room. Dust and dirt covered her left side, but angry fire blazed in her gold-flecked blue eyes. Nick felt himself grimace. He had no doubt that at least a small portion of that anger was directed at him. When he stepped closer, he saw the bruise on her fair skin.

"Dat close enough, Nick Price," Manno commanded. "You see she okay."

Clenching his fists, Nick ground his teeth then swallowed the rage welling inside of him. Cousan was definitely a dead man. "I'm here," he snapped from between clenched teeth. "Let her go."

Cousan chuckled. "Not yet. First we make sure the Vodun powers in you awake. Bernard!"

A short, white-haired black man emerged from behind a curtain.

Waving his hands, Cousan began pacing. "Bernard, he one of de true Vodun, one of de Council until dose fools afraid of der own power banish him. I welcomed Bernard. I believe in him and his power. Together we work in da shadows and show other Vodun dat life can be better, dat dey can have power in dis city."

Nick crossed his arms over his chest. "So what's that got to do with me?"

Cousan's arm-waving became more frantic. "I tol' you. De *Were* blood woke you power, made you stronger. I rule dis town den dis state wit yer help."

"I told you I wasn't interested."

Arms falling to his sides, Cousan stopped in mid stride. For a moment, he stared at Nick. Then he said, "Shoot de girl."

Before anyone could move, Nick answered in a calm tone, "Then you definitely won't get any cooperation from me. What's more, I'll hunt you down and kill you myself."

"You be dead too."

Nick shrugged. "Then the CIA will hunt you down. My aunt knows where I've come, and I've faxed my superiors. You sure you want to take on the CIA, Cousan?"

The taller man's eyes narrowed. "Dey nothing. Bernard, he take care of dem jus like dat." He snapped his fingers.

Nick curled his lip. "You sure you want to take the chance?"

"Stop wasting you time wit him, Manno," Bernard interrupted. "I jus take control of his powers, an' den he do what you want."

"Do it now!" Cousan demanded.

Before Nick could move, Bernard raised his hands, snapped his fingers and drew a circle with the index fingers of both hands. Then he pointed them at Nick. "Wake," he commanded. He began to chant in a low, guttural voice.

Inside Nick, the dark entity he'd been battling ever since his transfusion, the entity that had been riding close to his consciousness ever since he'd learned of Melody's capture, the one he'd thought defeated and banished with Melody's kiss, roared to life, embraced his body and infiltrated his mind.

Gasping and grabbing his head with both hands, he fell to the floor.

"Nick!" Melody screamed.

On his knees, Nick fought the devil inside his body—at least he tried to fight. The control he'd so prided himself on was stripped away. Blackness delved and twisted into every nook and cranny of his body and soul.

Bernard's chanting grew louder.

Nick twisted and groaned as he fought for control.

"You mine now!" Cousan crowed in triumph.

As the foul darkness washed through Nick and he felt his sense of being slip away, a long, wrath-filled howl split the air to be answered first by one then another and another until a chorus of anger bounced off the walls, floor and ceiling. Deep inside the darkness eating away at his soul, another entity howled in answer, a powerful, misty entity encased in silver, gold and ebony—not the oily, poisonous darkness currently racing through his body, but the clean blackness of a star-filled night. Expanding rapidly, it devoured the fiery evil clawing at his soul and filled Nick with the crisp, icy freshness of a moonless winter night.

As the pain melted and his clothing fell away, Nick rose to all fours and drew his lips back in a snarl. His blunt claws scratching the cement floor, he launched himself at his tormentor. From the other side of the room, mist dissipated and a silvery-white wolf leaped from the chair where Melody had been bound to join him in the attack. From the door he'd entered earlier, more wolves sprang.

Pivoting, Manno Cousan screamed once and fled through

a hidden door close to where he'd been standing. A large silver wolf shouldered both Melody and Nick out of the way and launched himself against the door. When it didn't budge, he howled with rage and tried to dig his way through.

A single gunshot echoed around the room, but Cousan's cronies fell screaming before the lupine onslaught.

Still waving his hands, Bernard fell screaming to the floor, pulled down by a large, iron-gray wolf mantled with the power of an Alpha.

Then a white light flashed around the room, its brightness momentarily blinding everyone.

"He is ours, André Bayon," an authoritative voice commanded.

Shaking his head, Nick blinked to clear his vision. At his side, Melody did the same.

Dark mist swirled, and the New Orleans Alpha stood before a group of nine brightly garbed humans led by a dignified, white-haired man the color of the deepest midnight.

"He helped murder *Were*," André answered as he wiped blood from his chin. "Why shouldn't I kill him?"

The white-haired man crossed his arms over his chest. "Because, Alpha, death is final. With us, he will suffer torments you cannot believe. He has murdered Vodun as well."

The Alpha looked down at the quivering man, spat on him, and turned away. Signaling to the Pack members who'd accompanied him, he said, "We go." Then he turned to Nick and Melody, who were still in wolf form. "You are welcome to join us." A scowl appeared on his face. "As are you, Brendan Gray, for the honor of your father and sister—and my mate. For me, you cannot leave New Orleans soon enough." The Alpha shifted and led his Pack from the room.

The silver wolf grinned a toothy smile but did not change to human.

As the group of Vodun took custody of Bernard, Nick's

aunt came to stand before him. Tilting her head to the side, she stared into his eyes. "De black flecks are gone. Your eyes are de gold of a true wolf." She shook her head. "I didn't believe it possible." Slipping to her knees, she wrapped her arms around his neck. "You are still my Nicholas, and I love you." Rising, she followed her cohorts from the room.

After she disappeared, Nick looked from Melody to her brother and back again. Opening his mouth, he tried to speak, but only a few harsh yips emerged.

Use your mind.

Nick stared at the silver-white wolf next to him. No sound had emerged into the air, but that comment had a definite femininity to it.

He formed his words in his mind as he continued to stare at Melody. *How the fuck do I change back to human?*

Chapter Twenty-One

ഩ

Leaning back in the comfortable leather chair, Nick steepled his fingers and stared at Melody. The anger he'd locked into a corner of his mind almost broke free as he gazed at the bruise on her face. If he ever got his hands on Cousan, he'd tear him limb from limb. Across the room, she smiled at him then turned her attention back to Noelle Bayon. He frowned. She looked calm and collected, but she was on edge, anxious. Why?

He shifted his attention to where Brendan talked with André next to the fireplace. Every now and then Melody's brother would toss a glare at Nick then refocus on the Alpha. Again, why?

A soft sigh trickled over his shoulder. "You have no idea what you're supposed to do, do you?" Noelle Bayon had left Melody and settled down into the chair next to his. Immediately, the tension that had meandered lazily around the room began to rise. André Bayon glared daggers at him. Brendan had a sneer on his face and Melody was frowning.

For his part, what Nick now recognized as his internal wolf, which was still trying to meld itself comfortably to his soul, raised its head to growl a warning when one of André's brothers stopped before Melody and began to speak to her. Nick's entire body tensed. What was that male doing sniffing around his mate?

Again Noelle sighed and placed her hand on Nick's arm.

A low growl rumbled from André and he took a step toward them.

"Males!" she snapped. "Stop acting like a fool, André! No one has explained anything to him!"

Across the room, Nick saw Melody stiffen. Her lips peeled back into a silent snarl.

Noelle waved her hand. "It's not your fault, Melody. He fled. You were kidnapped. There was no time. And, Henri, get away from her. You're asking for trouble."

Nick relaxed as the male joined the other two men. Why should he care if some guy talked to Melody?

Wrapping her fingers around his wrist, Noelle tugged him to his feet. "Come walk with me. We have a beautiful garden."

"Noelle!" André barked.

"If you say one more word, André," she snarled, "you will have a matching scar for the one you already have. You know there is no one for you but me." She patted her enlarged stomach. "As if this child I carry would allow for anything."

The Alpha's nostrils flared, but he didn't say a word.

Melody rose.

Noelle sighed.

"Stay, Melody." Noelle motioned to another woman in the room. "Annette, talk with Melody a bit then bring her to the garden."

As Noelle practically dragged him from the room, Nick looked back over his shoulder. Every gaze was following them. What the hell was going on? And why was this new wolf part of him so dead set against leaving Melody? If there weren't other women in the room, he wouldn't have gone. What the hell was the matter with him?

"*Mais*, it is hard for you, this change," Noelle said matter-of-factly as she led him through the mansion to a set of wide double doors that opened onto a magnificent garden.

"How would you know?" Nick mumbled.

Her chuckle was soft and—in some strange way—comforting. "My mother, she told me."

Nick turned and focused on her. "Your mother wasn't a

werewolf?"

Shaking her head, she answered. "No. You and I are now *Were*, werewolves, shape shifters, but there are many different kinds. Something for you to learn about later. Now you must concentrate on Melody."

"She's all I can think about," Nick grumbled.

They stopped walking and Noelle sank slowly and awkwardly onto a bench beneath a shady tree. "Forgive me, but I can't walk so far these days."

Nick focused his attention on his very pregnant companion. His experience with pregnant women was nonexistent. "Should I call someone?"

She chuckled. "Don't worry, I'm fine." She patted the bench next to her. "Sit. Listen."

Nick flopped down next to her, rested his elbows on his knees, laced his fingers together, and stared at the door through which they had come. Melody was supposed to come out here soon.

Noelle chuckled. "You watch for her, yes? Can't stop thinking about her, even when you want to?"

Nick simply growled.

She chuckled more. "It will never go away this longing for her, though you will learn to control it. The mating bond is strong, stronger than anything many humans ever experience. Yours is new—and incomplete."

Even as he asked, "What do you mean?" Nick remembered the kiss he'd shared with Melody in his aunt's house—was it only yesterday? That kiss had seemed to drag his soul from him, merge it with hers, then return to him in pieces with part of Melody's soul melded to his. How could anything get more complete than that?

"You haven't mated her yet."

Turning his head, Nick simply cocked an eyebrow and looked at her.

Again she chuckled. "*Mais*, sex and mating are two different things. In a true mating, the male dominates the female, makes her accept him. You must make her submit to you, mount her, make her yours."

Nick simply stared. "You mean, as wolves?"

She cocked her head to the side. "As humans, for it is our human sides that have to accept this bond. Our humanness fights against the wolf in us. For you, more so, since you have never known anything else." Again she placed her hand on his arm. "Learn to trust the wolf you have in you now. Wolves do not lie to themselves—ever."

Leaning back, she paused. "The female members of my family are Cajun witches. My mother fell in love with a *Were*. The mixing of their blood brought about the same change in her as it did in you. Since then, she has spent her life researching and studying the phenomenon. Normal humans accept a blood transfusion when they mate a *Were*. It gives them many of the characteristics of the *Were*, but they are not able to shift. For others, this is not always true. Vampires cannot change, nor do the Fae. Not all witches are able to do so, either. As far as we know, you are the first of Vodun blood to have a transfusion of *Were* blood, and you are able to shift."

"Are you going somewhere with this?"

Noelle sighed. "Forgive me. I keep forgetting your bond isn't completely forged yet. When Melody comes out, you must mate with her."

Nick snorted. "Just like that. With an audience?"

At that moment, Melody stepped out into the garden.

Their gazes locked.

Noelle rose. "Though it really wouldn't matter to you once the pursuit begins, you will be alone. The garden is three acres and walled for privacy. Run with her, pursue her, but in the end, you must make her accept your domination. Then your bond will be complete."

Nick didn't notice her leave. His senses were focused only

on Melody. Flaring his nostrils, he sniffed.

She was aroused.

His cock reacted immediately.

"Can't catch me," she said in a low sexy voice. Silvery mist formed. Her clothing fell to the ground. The white wolf was sprinting away from him before she was completely formed.

The internal entity that Nick was beginning to recognize as the wolf essence took command of his body. This time Nick didn't fight it. Tearing off his clothing, he shifted into wolf form and leaped after her.

The chase lasted far longer than Nick wanted. She was fast. Time and time again, she slipped away from him down carefully tended paths or through denser undergrowth. Finally, in a small, well-manicured clearing far from the house, he cornered her. Her back to the wall, she faced him on all fours, a snarl on her lips, sharp teeth displayed. Then silver mist exploded and she shifted to her human form.

Nick shifted seconds after she did. He was hot. He was tired. He'd chased her for over an hour. He wanted her. Now!

"Submit!" he demanded.

Her eyes widened then narrowed. "I am not a bitch in heat to come crawling to you."

A growl rumbled out of his chest. "You are mine."

She dodged left.

He blocked her retreat.

She dodged to the right, then quickly left again.

She almost escaped. Almost.

Turning, she leaped for the wall.

He grasped her around the waist and pulled her naked body against his. The aroma of her perspiration and perfume wound itself around him, and his cock rose, hard and aching. *Mate her,* Noelle Bayon had said. *Dominate her, make her accept you.*

As Melody struggled in his grasp, the tiny corner of Nick's logical, CIA-trained mind invaded his consciousness. *If domination means rape, you're better off dead. No real man would ever do that to a woman.*

His arms firmly wrapped around Melody's torso under her breasts, Nick closed his eyes. No matter what this new wolf part of him wanted to do, he would never force himself on Melody. He would rather be dead.

With a sigh, he let her go.

Spinning, lips pulled back in a snarl, she glared at him.

He waved his hand. "Go if you want. I care too much to force you. I could never do that to you."

Nick closed his eyes but it didn't matter. He could still see her perfectly. Once he'd thought her pale and almost colorless with her fair skin and white-blonde hair. What a fool he'd been. Her skin wasn't white like an albino. Normally, it was a warm ivory color. Flushed, it was pale pink. Her nipples were rosebuds. The hair curling over her cunt was blonde, white and silver all mixed together.

Christ, he thought to himself, *I sound like a fucking poet.*

"Nick?"

Her voice was soft.

He opened his eyes and watched her walk to him, her rose-nippled breasts bouncing slightly, her long hair swaying.

His cock jerked with each one of her steps.

The new wolf inside him howled and demanded that he take her.

Nick gritted his teeth and remained perfectly still. He would not be ruled by some animal instinct.

Melody stopped in front of him. "Nick," she said again as she wrapped her fingers around his cock and gave it a tug, "you could never hurt me. Take me. Now!" Leaning forward so that her breast brushed against his chest, she nipped the side of his neck—hard. Then she locked her mouth against his and sucked his tongue into her mouth.

The nip pushed him over the edge. Growling deep in his throat, he wrapped his arms around her and fell to the ground.

Locked in Nick's arms with her hands flat against his muscular chest, Melody attacked his mouth with hers. His suggestion that she leave him had simultaneously charmed and appalled her—charmed the human in her to know he cared, appalled the wolf in her to know he'd let her go. But she had him now, and judging by the rock-hard erection digging into her hip, he was more than ready for her—physically. But was he mentally ready for her?

Pulling his arms free, he rolled her over onto her back, pulled his mouth away from hers and immediately attacked her nipple.

Melody arched into his mouth as pleasure lanced straight to her groin. But this wasn't what she wanted or needed. Gathering all her strength, she pushed him off her and scrambled to her feet.

The howl of rage that erupted from Nick's throat when she escaped him sent shivers of anticipation up and down her spine. Just thinking of having him capture her again, dominate her, thrust his hard, black cock into her when he mounted her had her moaning with anticipation. Her stomach muscles clenched and moisture slid down the insides of her thighs.

"Don't play with me!"

"I like to play," she panted. "Don't you?" Cupping her breasts, she rolled her thumbs around her nipples then shuddered with pleasure. She was unable to stifle the moan.

"Stop teasing me, damn it! Do you want me or not?"

Almost, she thought. *Almost he's ready to let the wolf inside him take complete control.* Picking up a handful of loose mulch, she threw it at him. It bounced off his chest. At first, shock appeared on his face to be followed anger.

Melody turned to sprint away again.

She wasn't fast enough.

He tackled her to the ground, where she lay on his stomach with him on her back.

"I've had enough of this," he growled in her ear as she struggled to escape him. "First you have sex with me against a wall, then you strap me down to a bed and have sex with me again. You give me your blood and turn me into a half animal. You tell me I'm supposed to be your mate and chase me here to New Orleans where you get yourself kidnapped by an idiot who thinks he can use me to rule the world. I finally get my brain wrapped around everything and you run away? You tease me with the possibility of sex? Not this time, baby." He rose off her back, wrapped his arm around her waist, and pulled her up onto her knees. "Not now. Now, you are mine."

With those words, he thrust his cock as deeply into her body as he could.

Gasping, Melody shuddered as Nick's thick, heavy cock slid into her, stretched her, filled her. Unwrapping his arm, he placed his hand in the small of her back, bent one leg at the knee and planted his foot on the ground so he could slide as deeply into her as possible. Beneath him, Melody opened her mouth, moaned and began to pant. She slid her knees farther apart to give him greater access.

"Yes, oh yes," she moaned.

"You are mine," he growled as he pulled his cock free, slapped her ass, then rammed himself back into her.

Melody howled with joy. Her mate, Nick was her mate.

Grunting, Nick dug his toes into the soft grass, shoved his hips against her ass, and screwed his cock into her again. He pulled back out then rammed back into her again. Out again. In again. Her ass rose to meet his hips. Her ivory back glowed with perspiration. He could see her breasts swaying; her nipples brushed the ground. Then she fell to her forearms to give him deeper access.

His balls first bouncing then tightening and drawing up against his body, Nick twisted and swiveled and rotated his hips as he thrust his cock in, pulled it out, then thrust it back into her hot, wet cunt over and over. Never had he taken a woman so roughly, yet Melody was enjoying—no, glorying—in his dominating sexual attack. And it was an attack, one he couldn't believe he was making—or enjoying so much.

Yet she was enjoying it more.

Something in both of them was reaching out, melding, becoming one.

Nick slapped her ass again then watched his black cock slide between the dark red lips of her cunt. The slap he'd given her, though it hadn't been hard, remained as a red handprint on her ivory white skin. He screwed his hips against her ass and grunted as her internal muscles sucked him deeper into her body.

"Christ, baby," he muttered. "Christ."

"Harder, Nick. Fuck me harder," she moaned. "I want to come."

Another slap to her other ass cheek. "I know, baby, I know." Leaning over her back as he ground his cock into her, he slid his arm around her waist and slipped his fingers between her thighs. Moisture coated his finger and he began to rub her clit.

Another howl burst from her throat, and shivers rolled up and down Nick's spine. He'd never imagined anything as eerie as a wolf howl could sound so damned sexy.

"Are you ready, baby? Ready to come?"

"Yes, oh yes, oh yes!"

Nick was ready too. He pulled his hand from between her thighs and grabbed her waist with both hands. His cock was harder than it had ever been. His balls were ready to burst into fire. He pulled her ass back against his hips as he slammed himself into her again and again, faster and faster.

She ground her hips against him.

"Yes, oh yes, oh yes, oh yes!" A final feminine howl rent

the air.

Nick's own howl melted into hers as hot cum erupted from his balls and shot up his cock.

Moments later, as they lay in the grass, Melody snuggled in his arms, she looked up into his face and smiled.

Nick smiled back.

"Mine," she murmured as she kissed him on the mouth.

Chapter Twenty-Two

ℌ

Arms crossed, Nick watched as Melody once again hugged her sister Belle. They were nothing alike—at least physically. Where Melody was tall and blonde, Belle was short with dark, almost black hair. Personality-wise, though, they were very alike. Both of them were strong women.

The door opened and Belle's mate—would Nick ever get used to that word—Alex Whitehorse walked in and nodded to Nick.

Shifting his feet, Nick nodded back. Melody and he had arrived late yesterday afternoon after spending two days at Melody's cabin. His initial meeting with Belle and Alex had gone smoothly enough. The new sensitivity to his senses enabled Nick to not only identify other werewolves, but also to immediately know where each individual ranked in regard to the others around them. He was a quick study. The differences between Alphas, Betas, and others in the Pack hierarchy were clear to him.

Alex Whitehorse was an Alpha to be reckoned with.

Still, Nick was sure he could take him in a fight.

A knock on the door interrupted the sisters' talking. It was shoved open, and a short woman walked in followed by a tall, muscular man. Nick immediately stiffened.

It was Jake Hurley, the man he'd been chasing for the last two years. Except he wasn't Jake Hurley. He was Garth Gray, Melody's brother.

The big man's gaze locked with his. Everyone else was silent as he strode across the room, stopped in front of Nick and stuck out his hand. "Garth Gray. Welcome to the family."

Nick looked at the hand then looked at Melody. A slight smile twitched at the corners of her mouth. Nick sighed. He'd been off this particular case for almost two weeks now. Besides, there was no way he'd ever do any harm to Melody's brother. She'd tear him to pieces.

Grasping the proffered hand, Nick answered, "Nick Price. Glad to meet you—finally."

The other man grinned. "Soon enough for me. That's Eileen over with Belle and Melody. They've known each other since they were teenagers."

Nick nodded, but he didn't have the chance to say anything else. The door was pushed open and one of Alex's Betas stuck his head in the door. "Car coming."

"Dad's finally here," Belle said as she grabbed a hand of both Melody and Eileen.

Garth followed them out.

Alex looked at Nick, and for the first time Nick sensed uncertainty from him. "Shall we?"

"Have to sooner or later, I guess," Nick answered as he followed the others through the door and onto the wide porch. Alex stopped at his side.

A large SUV halted a short distance away. The driver's side door opened and Melody's brother Brendan stepped out. At Nick's side, Alex muttered, "Asshole."

Smiling, Nick shifted his feet. He was beginning to like this particular Alpha more all the time.

The passenger side door opened and another man who had to be Melody's father stepped out—Artemis Gray.

Nick tensed. At his side, Alex sucked in a breath. Power swirled around Melody's father and even from where he stood on the porch, Nick knew this was a man he would never mess with.

"Could you take him?" Alex whispered.

"Not even with your help," Nick answered in an equally

low voice.

Crossing his arms over his chest, Nick watched as first Belle then Melody and finally Eileen were swept into tight hugs. Grinning broadly, their father clapped Garth on the shoulder then pulled him into a hug also.

"Kearnan and Serena will be here tonight," Belle said in a voice loud enough for everyone to hear. "Come on, Dad, let Moira and the girls out. There's nothing here to hurt them."

Brendan shot a smartass grin first at Nick then at Alex before he opened the back door of the SUV.

"Cocksucker," Nick muttered.

Alex tossed a satisfied smile his way.

"Nick, Alex, my father, Artemis Gray," Belle said. "Dad, the one on the right is Alex, and on the left is Nick, Melody's mate."

The three men sized each other up, Melody's father staring first at one, then the other.

Tension rose.

Alex stuck his chin out.

Nick shifted his feet and shot a glance at Melody. He'd been trained to handle any situation, but meeting the werewolf father of his new mate was not in the training manual.

But before anyone could say anything, the word "challenge" echoed around the large clearing where the cabin sat. A half dozen werewolves appeared out of the surrounding forest in both human and wolf form and headed straight for the cabin.

Artemis turned as Nick followed Alex forward to the porch railing.

A large gray wolf was loping toward the cabin.

"Fuck!" Alex snarled.

Nick looked first to Alex then at his mate's father. Both men were concentrating on the approaching wolf. He glanced at Belle. She looked worried. He glanced at Melody. She looked apprehensive. The apprehension on her face was replaced with a puzzled expression. Finally, amazement followed quickly by anger spread over her face.

She gasped.

She cursed.

Finally she cursed again—loudly. Spitting out, "Damn that idiotic pain-in-the-ass," she snarled loudly as she strode across the clearing to meet the strange wolf. "Of all the pig-headed, idiotic, moronic stunts to pull! Damn it, Drake. How in the world did you find me? If I told you once, I told you a thousand times, I will not be your mate. I do not want to be your mate. I have found my mate, and he is not you. Now go away and leave me alone!"

Instead of answering, the big wolf dropped his head and closed his eyes. A gray mist appeared. Slowly, very, very slowly, the wolf melted away. Even more slowly, a man appeared in his place, a man who collapsed to the ground as soon as his transformation was complete.

At Alex's side, Nick growled, "Son of a bitch." Pushing Garth out of the way, he leaped off the porch and headed toward his mate.

Alex caught Belle's gaze.

She shrugged and shook her head. Obviously, she had no idea who this was.

Her brother Brendan threw back his head and laughed.

Fucking asshole, Alex thought. *One day I'm going to rip a few strips out of his hide—when Belle isn't around.*

"Melody, get back here," Nick growled as he stomped after her.

The man practically sprawling on the ground struggled to his feet and took one unsteady step toward Nick. "Stay away from my mate, or I will kill you."

Far more quickly than Nick had thought possible, Melody planted a quick jab in the stranger's midsection. As he doubled over and fell to the ground once again, she snarled, "Touch him, Drake, and I'll rip out your throat. *He* is my mate!"

Grabbing Melody's arm, Nick yanked her away from the stranger and took her place standing over him. New instincts were roaring through his brain, instincts that told him to protect his mate from this strange male—even by killing him if necessary. "She…is…mine. Leave, while you still have your life." Still clasping her arm, Nick turned and guided her back toward the cabin. His gaze locked with that of Melody's father. Ever so slightly, Artemis nodded his head with approval.

As Alex stalked past them, Nick turned to follow his progress. Now that he had Melody away from the stranger, he was curious to see what would happen.

"What do you want here?" the Alpha growled.

Sprawled on the ground, the stranger pushed himself up until he sat at the Alpha's feet. Every now and then, a tremor shook his body. He stared at Melody. "The first time I heard her howl, the music, the joy, the longing…" He shivered and blinked, pulled himself out of his memories. "I am Drake." He glanced back at Melody then stared at Nick. Finally, he refocused on Alex. "I thought I came for my mate. When she would not join me in the *Wilde*, I knew I had to give up my life of freedom and take this form again even though I had given it up many seasons ago." He looked to Melody again.

Nick snarled audibly.

Shoulders slumping, the stranger looked back at the Alpha. "She often told me she would not be my mate. In my pride I refused to believe." He lowered his head. "I ask for refuge, Alpha, until I regain my strength and am able to shift back. Then I will return to the *Wilde*."

Nick watched as the Alpha stared at the man named Drake. Then, slowly, he nodded. "Refuge is granted until you are able to shift without danger."

An elegant woman who had exited the SUV and now stood by Artemis Gray's side lifted herself on tiptoe and whispered in his ear. An eyebrow cocked up and he walked to Alex's side. "Drake?" he asked. "Prince Drake Vasilievich Meshchersky, son of prince Alexander Vasilievich Meshchersky and Princess Maria Natalia Meshcherskayou, who disappeared into the Alaskan wilderness?"

The stranger looked up. "Grandson. How did you know?"

"My wife has made a hobby of researching *Were* families with which the Hierarchy has lost contact."

Keeping his eyes on the man who'd come here looking for Melody, Nick made a mental note that her father referred to his mate as his wife. But then, according to what Melody had told him, his wife wasn't a real *Were* either.

Artemis reached down and offered the man named Drake his hand. "Your family left a sizable fortune in the care of the Hierarchy. Are you sure you want to return to the *Wilde*? As a human, you'll be very wealthy."

The man accepted the hand proffered to him. "Your name?"

"Artemis Gray," Melody's father answered.

As he pushed himself slowly to his feet, the other man nodded. "The wolves tell of you, the Alpha who left the *Wilde* with his cubs after his mate joined others on the moon paths."

Melody's father nodded as he steadied Drake. "I have mated again." He frowned. "How long has it been since you shifted? I didn't think you'd be able to hold it together."

Another tremor shook Drake. "Not since I was a cub."

"Idiot!" a new feminine voice snapped.

Nick jerked his head up as two new scents rode the breeze to his nostrils. The first was that of an older female who marched across the clearing toward them snarling orders left and right. "Don't just stand there! He needs help! Belle, get water. Alex, call off your watchers and Betas. This *Were* is in no condition to hurt anyone." She stopped in front of Melody's father. "And you, Artemis Gray, I would have thought *you* of all people would have more sense than to keep a *Were* who hadn't shifted since he was a cub standing naked on his feet this long."

"He just shifted a couple minutes ago, Alesandra," Alex snapped.

"He needs help now!" She motioned to the huge man at her side. "George, carry him back to my house."

Drake tried to protest, but his objections were brushed aside. The big man lifted the stranger in his arms and headed back the way he'd come with the woman barking more orders from his side.

Every wolf except those in Melody's immediate family leaped to obey her orders.

But Nick listened to her tirade with only part of his brain. Most of his attention was focused on the huge man at her side, a man who wasn't a man but who wasn't a werewolf either. Shock coursed through his body. The scent of bear surrounded him. *Werebear*? He looked at Melody.

She smiled. "I *told* you wolves weren't the only *Were.* You didn't believe me did you?"

"Learn something new every day, don't you?" Melody's brother Brendan said as he dropped a baby into Nick's arms.

Nick froze as a pair of sky blue eyes under a head of bright red hair looked up into his. The child's lips parted into a four-tooth smile, and she grabbed his nose.

"That's Myste," Brendan said. "The one with the dark hair is Raven."

Nick spared a quick glance at Melody. She was cooing at another little girl she held in her arms.

"They're our sisters," Brendan said matter-of-factly. "And this is Moira, Dad's mate—er, wife," he continued after she punched him in the ribs.

"Here, give her to me. Brendan likes to rattle other men by dropping the girls in their arms." She gave Melody's brother an amused smile. "He thinks he's always in control. One day, sooner or later, he's going to meet the right woman and all his famous control will be shot to pieces. He'll be whimpering like a cub caught in its first rainstorm."

The baby out of his arms, Nick relaxed. Smiling, he concentrated first on Moira. "I'm pleased to meet you." Then he turned his attention to Brendan. "I'm looking forward to the day you find *your* mate. I hope she's a real bitch."

Much later, Nick stretched out on the bed and watched as Melody removed her clothing. Her family wasn't so bad—for the most part. Even Brendan's twin brother Kearnan, who'd arrived with his mate Serena and daughter Morgan before dinner, was someone Nick could grow to like. If only Brendan weren't around. More than once, either Melody or Belle cuffed him for a comment he made. Black sheep. That's how he fit into this family. Troublemaker. Nick hoped he found a mate who made his life miserable—and lived on the other side of the world. Some place with lots of fleas.

Melody pulled him out of his musings. "Feel like a run in the woods?" Completely naked, she rose onto her toes and stretched her arms above her head. Her breasts rose and bobbed when she lowered her arms again. The scent of her arousal floated through the air.

Already naked, Nick leaped from the bed. Sweeping Melody into his arms, he tossed her onto the bed then leaped after her, covering her body with his, pinning her beneath him. "No, I do not want to run in the forest, in the grass, in the mountains, on the beach, or anywhere else that's outside. I want to stay right here—in this bed. We have had sex up against a wall, with me strapped to a hospital bed, in a garden in New Orleans, and in the woods behind your cabin—four times. Right now, I want to make love in a real bed just like normal people. I may be part werewolf now, but I was a human a lot longer. I like beds."

Melody looked up into his face and smiled. "I like beds

too." Lifting her head, she kissed him.

Sighing, Nick opened his mouth to her questing tongue. Kneeing her thighs apart, he slid his already aching cock into her. He groaned as her internal muscles latched onto him and sucked him deeper.

He groaned again.

Here in Melody's arms was where he belonged. Barging into her office that day not so long ago was the smartest thing he'd ever done.

Epilogue

ꟿ

Moira inhaled the scent of rich coffee as she walked into the kitchen. Hmm. Nothing like fresh brewed coffee to put her in a good frame of mind early in the morning.

Humming lightly, she grabbed a mug and poured herself some of the savory, dark liquid then sipped. No cream or sugar for her. She liked her coffee high test. Reaching up, she caressed the ivy growing in the pot on the kitchen window. It stretched, pushed out a few new leaves, and curled around her finger. She smiled. The *Were* blood she'd gotten from Artemis had awakened her dormant *Fae* powers. Plants followed her wherever she went. Flowers bloomed more sweetly, a definite plus since they relied solely on plants to make their perfumes.

Still smiling as she untangled her finger from the ivy, Moira sipped more coffee and gazed out her kitchen window only to shake her head as she spied a familiar figure striding across the backyard. Artemis! How had he managed to sneak out of the house without her knowing? She could have sworn he was still in bed. As she watched, he crossed the yard and patio to the sliding glass doors. There, he tapped lightly, a lopsided grin on his face.

Shaking her head, she walked across the kitchen and unlocked the door. When would this man learn not to go out the front door and expect to get in the back when the doors were locked?

He slid it open, stepped inside and closed it again against the morning chill.

"I thought you were still in bed," Moira murmured as she sidled closer. The scent of one of his signature colognes surrounded her. She inhaled. Artemis usually didn't put cologne on until he got dressed for work. It was Saturday and he wasn't going in today. Oh well, she so enjoyed how the scents of his colognes mixed with his own personal scent.

Setting her mug on the counter, Moira wrapped her arms around his neck and stretched her body up against his hard torso. She shivered. This man, this *Were* was more fascinating and exciting than anyone she'd ever met. As she raised her mouth, he lowered his. When their lips met, she sighed with satisfaction.

Almost immediately she stiffened. This close, she was able to smell his scent beneath the aroma of his cologne.

It was—strange, the same yet different.

His tongue played with hers in a new way.

This kiss was different.

This man was not Artemis!

Before she could push herself away, she was dragged from the man's arms and tossed somewhat gently across the kitchen. Then Artemis wrapped his fists in the stranger's shirt and threw him through the plate glass sliding doors. Glass shattered and skittered off the mosaic stonework of the patio as the stranger bounced then rolled to the verge of grass.

Still grinning that same lopsided grin, he pushed himself to his feet and began to brush the broken glass from his clothing. "You could have been a bit more gentle with your toss, brother."

"Touch her again and I'll rip out your throat," Artemis snarled. Hands fisted on his hips, he stood in the broken doorway, growls still rolling from his chest.

"Brother!" Moira exclaimed. She stomped to Artemis' side and looked at the man on the patio wincing as he pulled slivers of glass from his hair. A trickle of blood rolled down his cheek.

"Brother!" she exclaimed again. "You have a brother?" She looked from one identical face to the other. "A twin brother?" Spinning to face Artemis, she punched him in the ribs.

He didn't flinch. "Not now, Moira."

"Don't you 'Not now, Moira', me, Artemis Gray!" she snarled. "Why didn't you tell me you had a twin brother?"

"It wasn't necessary," he growled as he continued to glare at the other man. Then he added with a vicious snarl, "He kissed you."

Moira gaped at him then snapped her mouth closed. As her anger built, the various plants hanging about the kitchen began to sway. Stems, leaves and vines exploded as they sprouted haphazardly. Her voice echoed around the kitchen then fled through the shattered glass. The colorful flowers in ceramic pots began to sway and shake.

"Wasn't necessary! Kissed me! You idiotic blockhead! Did you ever stop to think that if you'd told me about him, he never would have gotten the chance to kiss me?" Spinning away from her husband, Moira stomped through the broken door, her hand extended.

He leaped after her. "Moira, get back in here."

She kept her back to him and ignored his command. "Go fly a kite!" She focused instead on her husband's brother. "Hello, I'm Moira. Please forgive Artemis." She shot a glare over her shoulder. "He can be such a blockhead at times."

Clasping the hand she held out to him and ignoring the deep growl that erupted from Artemis, he lifted it to his lips. "I'm well aware of my brother's shortcomings. I grew up with him. He always had something of a short temper." He kissed the back of her hand lingeringly.

Another louder, deeper growl erupted from Artemis.

His brother let go of her hand but his gaze remained locked on hers. "Tristan Gray. Sorry it's a bit late, but congratulations on your nuptials and welcome to the family."

Moira shook her head. She was talking to an older version of Brendan. "Men," she said with a sigh. "With you for an uncle, I understand Brendan completely now."

Throwing back his head, Tristan laughed long and loud.

Still shaking her head, Moira tucked her hand under Tristan's arm. "Come in and let me take care of that cut on your head." She glared at Artemis. "You have a mess to clean up."

He didn't move from where he blocked the door.

Moira stopped, pulled herself to her full five-feet-five-inch height and stated in a clear voice, "I swear, Artemis Gray, if you don't move, you'll regret it until your dying day."

Slowly he back away and allowed Moira to lead his brother into the kitchen. Once she stepped in the door, the baby monitor light blinked and the sound of both daughters fussing reached her. Tsking, she pushed Tristan down into a chair and turned to Artemis. "If he isn't sitting in that chair—in one piece—when I get down here..."

After one last glare, she hurried from the kitchen.

"She is worthy of you, brother."

With Moira gone, Artemis forced himself to relax. "You should know better than to kiss another wolf's mate, especially mine."

Grinning, Tristan shrugged. "She kissed me first. Thought I was you. It's not the first time that's happened."

Grabbing the coffee pot, Artemis snorted. He should have told Moira about his brother. He'd just never found the right time. He glanced at Tristan. Damn, but Brendan was becoming more and more like him every day. Surely he'd find a mate to settle him down soon. Artemis signed. Unless Brendan was truly like Tristan. His brother had never found a mate. Maybe that was also Brendan's fate.

Turning, Artemis handed his brother a cup of coffee.

"Why did you send for me?" Tristan asked as he accepted the mug his brother held out to him.

All thoughts of Brendan fled from Artemis' mind and a

frown appeared on his face. "Melody was kidnapped."

Mug halfway to his mouth, Tristan froze. His words were low and dangerous. "She is free?"

Artemis nodded. "Brendan and her mate freed her."

Tristan cocked an eyebrow. "Mate?"

Artemis smiled. "I'll let Moira tell you all about it."

"The kidnapper?" Steam curled from the hot coffee toward the ceiling.

Artemis gulped the coffee he held. "Escaped."

Flaring his nostrils, Tristan barked, "Where?"

"New Orleans."

"The Pack Alpha?" Tristan continued to ignore his coffee.

"Will cooperate," Artemis answered. "This man, Manno Cousan, has murdered Pack members, but they haven't been able to catch him."

"The Hierarchy?"

"All agree. Cousan has kidnapped and murdered *Were*. There is only one answer for his transgressions."

Tristan nodded and waited.

Artemis looked him straight in the eye. "Hunter, you are unleashed."

Also by Judy Mays

ꕥ

eBooks:

Celestial Passions 1: Brianna

Celestial Passions 2: Sheala

Celestial Passions 3: Meri

Fires of Solstice

Heat: A Midsummer Night's Heat

Heat: In the Heat of the Night

Heat: Perfumed Heat

Heat: Solstice Heat

Rednecks 'n' Rock Candy

Rednecks 'n' Roses

Undercover Heat

Print Books:

A Breath of Heat

A Touch of Heat

Celestial Passions 1: Brianna

Celestial Passions 2: Sheala

Fires of Solstice

Rednecks 'n' Romance

About the Author

ꟹ

Foxier than a Hollywood starlete! More buxom than a Vegas showgirl! Able to undangle participles with a single key stroke!

Look! At the computer!

It's a programmer!

It's a computer nerd!

No! It's—Judy Mays!

Yes, Judy Mays—Romantica™ writer extraordinaire who came to Earth with powers and abilities far beyond those of mortal writers. Judy Mays! Who can write wild, wanton werewolves, assertive, alluring aliens and vexing, vivacious vamps. Who, disguised as a mild-mannered English teacher in a small Pennsylvania high school, fights a never-ending battle for Heroic Hunks, Hot Heroines, and Sexy Sensuality!

Judy welcomes comments from readers. You can find her website and email address on her author bio page at www.ellorascave.com.

Tell Us What You Think

We appreciate hearing reader opinions about our books. You can email us at Comments@EllorasCave.com.

Why an electronic book?

We live in the Information Age—an exciting time in the history of human civilization, in which technology rules supreme and continues to progress in leaps and bounds every minute of every day. For a multitude of reasons, more and more avid literary fans are opting to purchase e-books instead of paper books. The question from those not yet initiated into the world of electronic reading is simply: *Why?*

1. ***Price.*** An electronic title at Ellora's Cave Publishing and Cerridwen Press runs anywhere from 40% to 75% less than the cover price of the exact same title in paperback format. Why? Basic mathematics and cost. It is less expensive to publish an e-book (no paper and printing, no warehousing and shipping) than it is to publish a paperback, so the savings are passed along to the consumer.
2. ***Space.*** Running out of room in your house for your books? That is one worry you will never have with electronic books. For a low one-time cost, you can purchase a handheld device specifically designed for e-reading. Many e-readers have large, convenient screens for viewing. Better yet, hundreds of titles can be stored within your new library—on a single microchip. There are a variety of e-readers from different manufacturers. You can also read e-books on your PC or laptop computer. (Please note that Ellora's Cave does not endorse any specific brands.

You can check our websites at www.ellorascave.com or www.cerridwenpress.com for information we make available to new consumers.)

3. ***Mobility.*** Because your new e-library consists of only a microchip within a small, easily transportable e-reader, your entire cache of books can be taken with you wherever you go.
4. ***Personal Viewing Preferences.*** Are the words you are currently reading too small? Too large? Too... ANNOYING? Paperback books cannot be modified according to personal preferences, but e-books can.
5. ***Instant Gratification.*** Is it the middle of the night and all the bookstores near you are closed? Are you tired of waiting days, sometimes weeks, for bookstores to ship the novels you bought? Ellora's Cave Publishing sells instantaneous downloads twenty-four hours a day, seven days a week, every day of the year. Our webstore is never closed. Our e-book delivery system is 100% automated, meaning your order is filled as soon as you pay for it.

Those are a few of the top reasons why electronic books are replacing paperbacks for many avid readers.

As always, Ellora's Cave and Cerridwen Press welcome your questions and comments. We invite you to email us at Comments@ellorascave.com or write to us directly at Ellora's Cave Publishing Inc., 1056 Home Avenue, Akron, OH 44310-3502.

ELLORA'S CAVE
ROMANTICA PUBLISHING

Breinigsville, PA USA
30 November 2010

250360BV00002B/23/P